HALF WORLD

HALF WORLD

HIROMI GOTO

illustrations by JILLIAN TAMAKI

VIKING

An Imprint of Penguin Group (USA) Inc.

VIKING
Published by Penguin Group
Penguin Group (USA) Inc., 345 Hudson Street, New York, New York 10014, U.S.A.
Penguin Group (Canada), 90 Eglinton Avenue East, Suite 700, Toronto, Ontario, Canada M4P 2Y3
(a division of Pearson Penguin Canada Inc.)
Penguin Books Ltd., 80 Strand, London WC2R 0RL, England
Penguin Ireland, 25 St Stephen's Green, Dublin 2, Ireland (a division of Penguin Books Ltd.)
Penguin Group (Australia), 250 Camberwell Road, Camberwell, Victoria 3124, Australia
(a division of Pearson Australia Group Pty Ltd.)
Penguin Books India Pvt. Ltd., 11 Community Centre, Panchsheel Park, New Delhi—110 017, India
Penguin Group (NZ), 67 Apollo Drive, Rosedale, North Shore 0632, New Zealand
(a division of Pearson New Zealand Ltd.)
Penguin Books (South Africa) (Pty) Ltd, 24 Sturdee Avenue,
Rosebank, Johannesburg 2196, South Africa

Penguin Books Ltd., Registered Offices: 80 Strand, London WC2R 0RL, England

First published in slightly different form by Puffin Canada, 2009.
This edition first published in the United States of America in 2010 by Viking,
a member of Penguin Group (USA) Inc.

1 3 5 7 9 10 8 6 4 2

Text copyright © Hiromi Goto, 2009, 2010
Illustrations copyright © Jillian Tamaki, 2009

LIBRARY OF CONGRESS CATALOGING-IN-PUBLICATION DATA IS AVAILABLE
ISBN 978-0-670-01220-6

Printed in U.S.A.
Set in Aurelia EF
Book design by Kate Renner

For my mother, Kyoko Goto, for showing me that soft power endures, has the wisdom and capacity to bend . . . *Subarashii.*

HALF WORLD

PROLOGUE

LONG, LONG, LONG ago, before mortals began to inscribe mortal religions onto stone tablets and parchment, there was a time of the Three Realms: the Realm of Flesh, the Realm of Spirit, and Half World.

For eons it was a time of wholeness and balance; Life, After Life, and Half Life were as natural as awake, asleep, and dreaming. All living things died only to awaken in the dream land of Half World. Mortals awoke to the moment of the greatest trauma they had experienced during their time in the Realm of Flesh. In Half World they relived Half Lives, until they had worked through their burdens of mortal ills, through trial and tribulation. Wrongdoings, doubts, fears, terror, pain, hatred, suffering, all the ills of mortality had to be integrated and resolved before they could rise from mortal fetters into light and Spirit. Once in the Realm of Spirit, all physical cares disappeared. Spirits existed freely, unbounded by mortality and suffering, untroubled by Flesh, in a state pure and holy. Until eventually their light began to grow dim, and they were called back into Flesh once more. For without connections to Life, Spirit, too, shall pass away.

Thus, the cycles were in balance.

There is no account left of what led to the severing of the Realms. No one knows if it was the work of Spirits who grew aloof and righteous, if it was a trapped Half Worlder maddened into perpetual pain with no hope left of light.

Perhaps it was a mortal who dreamt of becoming a Spirit without ever leaving Flesh. But the Three Realms that were once balanced and entwined were ripped asunder and locked into isolation.

Mortals, caught in perpetual mortality, died only to be born again into Flesh. Trapped in this unchanging cycle, they grew bleak and despairing. Violence, wars, environmental destruction accreted as time passed. When they died, the mortals' Half Spirits could not move on to Half World. Instead, they were born back into Flesh without ever transcending their suffering. With no Half World to work through their troubles and no Spirit to raise them, mortals descended ever deeper into suffering. Atrocities proliferated and hope began to fade.

Half World, locked into ceaseless psychic suffering with no chance of redemption, spiraled into madness. There was no life in Half World and no death. None were born and no one died. Never meant to be fixed into perpetuity, the transformative powers of Half World morphed into nightmare proportions.

The Spirits, cut off from mortality and Flesh, began losing all memory, all knowledge of the other Realms. Growing cooler and more distant, they forgot they were part of a greater pattern.

Their lights are beginning to fade, slowly, one by one. . . . They have not enough left to them to even care.

The Three Realms are in great peril. The Realms are very close to dissolution.

It is said that when the impossible happens, when a living infant is born into Half World, only then will the fate of the Realms be altered. In a Realm without birth or death, where none are truly living, the cycles of perpetual suffering have shaped monsters. From this unchanging nightmare can anything be born?

The birth of a living child is the doom and hope of Half World.

But millennia have passed and this child has yet to be born.

—a fragment from what has been called
THE BOOK OF THE REALMS

INTRODUCTION

THE WOMAN, HEAVY with child, clasped a desperate arm around the curve of her belly as she ran along the fragile black bridge. Her male companion kept pace slightly behind her, one hand extended in case she should stumble. The woman's breath rasped with terror, pain, exhaustion. Icy air numbed their senses. They ran, refusing to look downward at the great empty chasm below. So very deep, if they fell they would never reach the bottom. A few wisps of clouds trailed beautifully far below them. The insubstantial surface bridged the gap between the Realms, and they could see the cliff that was purported to hide the Gate to the other side. So close. A world away. They ran, breath choking their throats, pain stabbing their sides, emptiness yawning all around them. With each desperate step they took, the rail-less bridge undulated and wobbled, swayed and fluttered.

The terrifying plummet one misplaced foot away.

"Faster," her male companion pleaded, casting a look over his shoulder. The pursuers were gaining on them, sly, chortling, hopping, creaking.

"Be careful!" a sticky voice shouted. "Don't slip and faaaallllll!"

The woman made a harsh sound and somehow increased her pace.

"Oh, wait," the sticky voice wheedled, like a younger brother. "Wait for meeeeeeeeeee!"

They reached the rocky ledge, the gray of stone. Panting, sobbing with relief at feeling solid rock beneath their feet, they didn't notice the crunch of dry little sticks snapping under their weight.

"What must we do now?" the woman gasped. Patting the cliff face with desperate hands, she stared fearfully over her shoulders. Their enemies were almost upon them.

The man just shook his head, incapable of speech.

The pregnant woman smacked at the wall of rock. "Open!" she shouted. "Open!"

Something creaked with the slow weight of granite. With a great groan a giant wrenched free of her mountain prison and the cliff ledge shook, small stones tumbling, as the Gatekeeper stiffly stepped out of the wall. Over ten feet tall, she gazed across the great divide with gray stone eyes the same color as her entire body. "You must pay the toll in order to pass," her low voice rumbled.

The woman and the man looked up to stare upon a timeless stone face, cracked and dry. She did not look down, but only continued gazing across the chasm.

"Your time wanes." Her voice was expressionless. Neutral.

The woman fell to the giant Gatekeeper's feet. "Please. I beg you. Let us pass!"

The Gatekeeper remained silent.

Something white, gluey, and elastic smacked and adhered to

the rock face, a long strand stretching, intact, from the point of origin.

The woman and man looked back.

"Ehhht. Aiii hahheiiiii," the gluey man garbled as he strode the last few steps toward them, his elongated tongue growing shorter and shorter as he drew nearer. He stopped, and the tip of his tongue popped off the rock face with a wet sound, snapping back into his mouth. He fastidiously spat out little shards of rock.

Tall, thin, and reeking acrid and moldy, their enemy grinned at them with a mouth loose and elastic. His tiny pinprick pupils were black beads in the large whites of his eyes, and his tangled white hair stunk of vinegar. He was dressed in an overlarge raincoat, his thin legs sticking out from the bottom and large rubber boots rattling around his skinny calves. He opened his raincoat and fluttered the lapels, a wet, sour cloud billowing outward.

The man and woman each clamped a hand over their mouths as they began to cough.

The stinking man shook one boot, and putrid fumes rose upward. "I do so hate running in these things," he whispered. "I'm so hot I'm melting!" The inside of his mouth dripped downward, gooey and soft, threatening to spill from his thin lips. He sucked the gluey whiteness inward with a squelching slurp.

The man and the woman shuddered as the last of his gulping and gibbering friends stepped off the path to crowd upon the twig-strewn ledge. A fish-headed child, too close to the edge, windmilled thin arms as vertigo pulled her backward. "Ow! Ow! Ow!" she cried.

The reeking man in the raincoat giggled, then puckered his loose lips like a kiss. He blew. The sour breath hit the child in the chest and she toppled in slow motion backward into the gawping abyss. Her shrieks took ever so long to fade.

The motley creatures hooted and guffawed, hopping up and down on kangaroo legs, swinging reptilian tails and clapping their strangely formed hands.

"Please," the woman begged their leader. "Let us pass into the Realm of Flesh. We shall harm nothing of the workings of Half World once we are gone."

The man in the raincoat cupped his right elbow with his left hand, his fingers tapping his tacky cheek thoughtfully. "Maaaaay-beeee," he crooned in a childish voice, slumping his weight onto one hip. "Maybe not!" He swung out his opposite hip. He began tossing his hips in time with his response. "Maybe, maybe not! Maybe, maybe not! Yes! No! Maybe so! Yes!No!Maybeso! Yes! No! MAYBE SO!" he roared.

The young couple cowered at his feet.

The Gatekeeper stared implacably across the great divide.

The reeking man sighed, as if he were troubled. "How about this," he suggested, his tone moderate and kindly. "I like to play games. Doesn't everyone love games?"

"Yes, yes, we all love games," his motley companions agreed fawningly.

"Shut up!" he roared, and the companions reared back, a few dangerously close to the edge.

"As I was saying," he continued, gazing with compassion at the young couple, "this particular game has concluded with my victory. One point for me, zero for you. But if I drag you back with me it will be back to the ol' cycle. And I've grown so tired of the routine." He yawned dramatically. Body temperature cooling, the inside of his mouth no longer sagged like melting cheese. "I know!" he shrieked like an excited child. The young couple flinched.

"I know! I know! Ask me what!" he demanded.

The young couple obeyed. "What?"

"What, please!" the stinking man screamed.

"What, please," the pregnant woman said wearily.

"You"—he pointed at her—"I will allow to pass. But you will leave your little love bucket behind." The reeking man gazed pityingly at the young man. "Ahhhhh," he crooned. "Thus sweet, tender love parted." He wiped an imaginary tear from the corner of his eye. "I will hold him ransom. I give you fourteen years of maternal bliss and life to enjoy your love whelp in the Realm of Flesh. But when I tell you to return, you will bring the child back with you for a lovely family reunion. If you do not return, I will flay your lover every day and force him to eat his skin, for all eternity." He stretched his neck down, down, to press his tacky nose against the woman's horrified face. "Do you agree?"

The woman wrapped both arms around her middle. She turned to gaze upon the ashen face of her love.

"Go," the young man said hoarsely. "We have no other choice. If you remain we have nothing at all, we will fall back into the pattern. But this"—he cupped one hand wonderingly over the bulge of the unborn baby—"this is something new. . . . Go! Fourteen years is something even if it all comes to naught." He pressed his face into his love's hair as if he were kissing her for the last time. "You needn't return," he whispered.

The woman reared away from his words, her eyes full of tears.

"Yes!" The stinking man clapped his hands with a wet squelch. "They're going to take door number four!"

His companions hooted and clapped.

"The toll," the Gatekeeper groaned.

The young woman and the man stared fearfully at each other, patting their pockets for coins, food, anything.

The reeking man in the raincoat covered his lips with his hand and began to titter.

"We have nothing," the young couple beseeched.

"The toll is the smallest finger of your hand," the Gatekeeper intoned.

"Better and better!" the man in the raincoat chortled. "Don't you love this part?" he asked his companions. They began to clap, enthusiastically, once more.

"*Shhhhhht!*" he admonished. "I can't hear!"

The young couple gazed at their pale hands. They looked about for a piece of rock with a sharp edge, with which to cut. Stopped. They finally saw that the small, dry twigs beneath their feet were the bones of those who had tried to pass long, long ago.

"The finger must be bitten off," the Gatekeeper intoned.

The young woman held up her trembling hand. She curled her fingers around her thumb, leaving her pinkie extended. "Bite it off," she demanded, gritting her teeth. "Do it!"

Her companion opened his mouth and gently placed the edge of his teeth against the thin layer of flesh. Tears streamed down his face as he began to apply pressure.

He fell back. "I can't," he sobbed, hands covering his face. "I can't do it."

"He can't do it!" the man in the raincoat repeated gleefully.

The young man lowered his hands and extended his pinkie toward his love. "Take mine," he said.

The young woman's haggard face shone with love and sorrow. Her dark eyes narrowed. She grabbed his hand and bit down on his pinkie, hard, fast, a wet crunch. Dark blood filled her mouth, and the young man swallowed a scream, then fell backward in a faint.

"She did it," the man in the raincoat said with wonder.

"Ohhhhhhhhhh," his companions sighed.

The young woman's eyes welled with guilt and love. She spat out her lover's pinkie into her palm. She tipped her hand and the finger fell to the ground.

The great rock face creaked and groaned as a portal slowly ground open.

The man in the raincoat did not stop her. "Buh-bye!" he called out merrily. "Fourteen years, sweetheart. Be very brave! We'll be thinking about you. Don't worry about your love bucket. We won't drop him when we cross over the bridge. We'd never do a thing like that! Don't worry! Have a nice tiiiiiiiiiime!"

The woman stepped through.

She did not look back.

The portal closed with a grinding sound like a millstone.

ONE

MELANIE TAMAKI PELTED around the corner of the damp sidewalk in front of Rainbow Market. The worn soles of her runners slipping on a wet leaf, she almost fell, but she managed to keep her balance and staggered on.

Something hit her square in the back.

Soft. Squishy. Probably a tomato.

Panting, gasping, Melanie kept on running. She was lucky it wasn't an apple. Apples left bruises. She knew through experience.

"Come back, retard!" a voice jeered.

"Fat crow!" another voice screamed. "We're gonna get you!"

"Lookit her ass move!" they shrieked, teeth gleaming like wolves.

Four, five girls were chasing her. Off the school grounds. Onto the streets.

"Hey!" Melanie heard an old woman's voice bellow. "Leave her alone! Calling the cops on hooligans and miscreants!"

Despite the fear in her throat, warmth swelled in Melanie's eyes.

Ms. Wei was always nice to her. Even when it meant that her store would be vandalized on Halloween.

Melanie kept on running, her body heavy, her sides stabbing

with pain. She could hear the echo of her tormentors' footsteps pounding behind her, though it sounded like they were slowing down, losing interest.

A tiny portion of her mind gazed upon her flight with detached humor. What a waste of effort, she thought. If only her gym teacher could time this run, her P.E. marks would go up . . .

When she finally pattered to a stop, she was trembling with exhaustion and far beyond her neighborhood.

Her tormentors were gone.

Panting, gasping, Melanie bent over, almost retching. Her knees quivered with fear and exhaustion, and her long black hair clung wet with sweat. She pushed her straggly hair behind her ears and sat down on the curb. Waited, breathed, willing her pounding heart to slow.

Melanie gave a ragged sigh.

There was no point in going back to school. The Valkyries might be waiting for her by the parking lot, and she'd miss most of her Math Essentials, anyway, before ever getting through the door. After that there was only gym . . . she was too exhausted to run any laps, and she'd only get in trouble for being a slacker. The kids would make fun of her some more.

Melanie dragged her sleeve under her nose. Was there enough time to take the bus to the used bookstore downtown and get back home before her mum worried?

Melanie loved Macleod's. Its leaning towers of dusty books teetering up to the ceilings, the mounds of ragged tomes, a great many of them uninteresting and boring, but sometimes among them a wondrous discovery, like an amazingly illustrated anthology of medieval creatures. Or a cookbook from an ancient emperor's banquet. Or a travel-worn volume of edible plants in Patagonia, complete with photographs. . . . The children's section wasn't really up to date, but Melanie mostly liked to look at nonfiction books with illustrations and read the descriptions.

When she had shared her fondness for old books with a radical substitute teacher, she had heard about the store on the edges of a more ragged part of the city. It wasn't the safest area, Ms. Lee cautioned, but most people there did no harm except to themselves. Far more dangerous, she warned, were the people who preyed upon them. Under advisement to go only during the day, Melanie had ventured to the bookstore one rainy Saturday.

And fell in love with the entire place.

It wasn't only the scavenger hunt aspect of the books—she was also intrigued by the quiet people she saw there. In interesting clothing and odd hats, they looked like they had strange and extraordinary private lives, something beyond the mind-numbing routines of school and work.

She never saw any of her classmates at Macleod's.

Melanie squinted at the sun as it moved through patches of dark gray clouds. It was probably too late to get downtown and back before her mother began to wonder where she was. And she would get caught by the early rush hour. Her mum had looked particularly wan this morning. There was no need to add to her exhaustion unnecessarily, Melanie decided. She would go to the small park near the train tracks, her other special place. She would rest there for a little while, before going home.

◉

Melanie sat on an old, disused dock, swinging her dangling feet as she stared across the dirty gray water of the inlet. Light speckled over the surface, as the sun moved in and out of clouds. The tide was pushing a yellow plastic bag toward the edge of the rocky shore, which glinted with shards of broken bottles, crumpled aluminum cans. Tankers, silent and inexorable, crept toward the industrial docks. Melanie shivered as the afternoon grew chillier.

Crack! Something fell on a large rock near her and Melanie flinched.

Her heart began to pound.

Had her tormentors discovered her sanctuary? Were they throwing stones?

It was a mussel, shell broken, its pale, wet insides glistening.

Melanie cast furtive looks all around her, but she could see no one. Where did it come from? She frowned, then looked up just as a crow spiraled down. It landed with a swish of wings and hopped toward its prize. It stopped, before reaching the exposed mussel, and tilted its head to one side to peer with one glinting eye at the girl. Melanie gave it a lopsided grin. "Hello, crow friend," she murmured.

Melanie didn't know if the crows began loving her first or if her love had called the crows, but whenever she ventured outdoors they were nearby. As far back as she could remember. Perched on treetops, on the roof of a building across the street, her dark guardians were never far. The smile fell from her face.

Melanie turned to the water once more and stared at the distant shore. Industrial cranes, with their bright orange legs and long necks, looked like mechanical giraffes. In her peripheral

vision she could see the crow hop closer and begin picking at its meal. Melanie's stomach grumbled. She was hungry . . . almost hungry enough to try the abundant mussels exposed on the rocks, but she knew the water was filthy with chemicals, tanker sludge, and heavy metals. "It's not good for you," she murmured to the crow.

Melanie was very hungry. The fridge had been emptied two days ago, and they had finished the last box of instant mashed potatoes the night before. It wasn't her mum's fault. Melanie blinked. She raised her legs and rested her cheek upon her knees, her black hair falling across her face.

Her mum wasn't well, had never been healthy and strong. Her complexion was always wan, and the dark circles underneath her eyes never faded. She couldn't keep a job for longer than a few months before her body broke and she had to rest in bed for several weeks. For a while Melanie had worried that her mum had leukemia or cancer, maybe AIDS, but when she forced her to go to a clinic all the tests turned out negative.

The past three years her mother had turned to drink. . . .

Melanie sniffed. The material of her jeans smelled slightly sweet, like the fur of a cat come in from the cold. It was time to do laundry.

Melanie knew it was a hard life to be a single mother. In all her memories her mother had been there, never leaving her side. Her mum had never taken a lover; she never had a boyfriend or girlfriend. When Melanie had asked her why, her mum had smiled sadly. "I'm waiting for the day when I'll see your father once more."

Melanie had been happy to hear that when she was little, but as the years passed and her father never materialized she realized he was probably dead. Her mother had never answered any questions about her father—who he was, where he lived, how they had met. Her mother's eyes would fill with tears, and Melanie would only feel terrible for making her cry. There were many things that her mother couldn't tell her, and as time passed, and her mother grew weaker, the problems of the present, like money for groceries, became more pressing.

Were they in a witness protection program?

You're the best thing that's happened to me for all time, her mum had told Melanie her entire life. She still believed her.

Her cold nose beginning to run, Melanie sniffed again.

Crack, crack, smack! More mussels fell from the sky and crows gathered for their feast. Melanie glanced at them with envy. If all she had to worry about was finding enough food to fill her stomach for one day, what a simple life it would be.... The teachers had written her off at school, and she'd been streamed into the non-academic lot along with most of the other low-income students. So there was very little pressure for her to do much academically. That didn't stop the Valkyries from hazing her every day. And her mum was slowly fading away, as if there were hardly anything of her left.

Melanie shook her head. My mum is not dying! she thought fiercely. And I can quit school in a couple of years to get a full-time job. Maybe she could find a part-time job in the neighborhood, for after school and the weekend. They didn't own a lawnmower, and she'd never babysat before, but she could do something like walk rich people's dogs. Dog walkers didn't have to have nice clothes. . . .

Maybe she should start the long walk home and stop by to chat with Ms. Wei at Rainbow Market. She wanted to thank her, and maybe, if the store wasn't so busy, she could ask her only friend for some advice. Ms. Wei was not one to proffer advice and Melanie had never asked her for any, but the old woman had seen a lot of life. Over the years Ms. Wei had shared some of her life experiences with her. She might have some good ideas.

Something fell with a hollow *tock* upon the gray slats of the old dock. It didn't at all sound like a mussel. Melanie glanced down.

It was a fortune cookie. Neatly split in half. The end of a strip of pink paper fluttered. Melanie looked upward. High above, a crow made a slow, wide spiral. How peculiar, she thought. From that height the cookie should have shattered into bits.

The bird cawed once, then flew westward. Melanie reached out and pinched the fortune between her thumb and forefinger. She gently tugged it sideways out of its cookie shell and flattened the slightly furled strip of paper upon her thigh.

Melanie's breath caught in her throat. The crows on the beach had gone silent. They all stared at her with tilted heads, with one dark and glistening eye. Melanie's heart pounded in her ears.

What did it mean? It was just coincidence. It wasn't a *message* message meant for her.

"Hahahahaha," she laughed weakly, for her own benefit.

The dark birds burst upward with a rush of wings. They flew hard and fast toward the west, after the message-bearing crow.

Fat droplets of rain began to fall.

Melanie leapt to her feet, her heart pounding in her chest. The *plip, plop* of rain slowly accelerated into a low roar.

Melanie thrust the fortune into her jacket pocket.

She began to run.

TWO

MELANIE WAS EXHAUSTED by the time she passed Ms. Wei's corner store at a slow, plodding jog. The sudden rainstorm had darkened the afternoon, and the warm light shining from the Rainbow Market sent a pang of longing inside Melanie's heart. She did not stop. Her exhausted feet slipped atop slick wet leaves and she almost fell, catching her balance only at the last moment.

The few people who were out in the rain stepped far to the side to get out of the way of the stumbling girl.

Staggering through the rickety fence of their wretched rented house, Melanie didn't notice two crows sitting atop the cedar-shingled roof.

She stopped.

The front door was ajar. And though dusk gathered the darkness, no lights shone from the windows.

Her mum had been home, in bed, when she left her in the morning.

It hadn't been such a bad morning that her mum had to stay in bed all day.

She should be up, in the living room or the kitchen. For their after-school cup of hot tea.

Melanie crept up the three rotting steps, her breathing over-loud, labored.

She entered the doorway and stood on the muddy mat.

The house was cold and dark.

"Mum?" Melanie called out, her voice quavering. She reached out to flick on the living room lights.

Her mum was not there.

Melanie's heart thumped inside the hollow of her chest. "Lucka, lucka, lucka," she chanted childishly under her breath. "Lucka, lucka, lucka, lucka, lucka . . ."

That she wasn't there was both good and bad. Because she could be there, but dead. Killed. They didn't live in the safest neighborhood. Or she could have given up, weak. Then drank too much on top of it. Ended up dead. Then it would be better if she weren't there at all. Better to be alive, somewhere else, than there, but dead. Better to be gone. But then she might have been abducted. Or run away. Finally abandoned her troublesome daughter to find her missing love. She might still be alive, good, but have run away from Melanie. Bad.

Melanie clasped her arms around her soft middle. Shut up, she thought. Shut up and look!

The kitchen was empty. The kettle unplugged. The tea things were on the counter. Like her mother had set them out, waiting for her daughter's return.

But where had she gone?

Melanie creaked across the dirty floor toward the hallway. In the bathroom the leaking faucet pattered its incessant dribble.

Her mother was not there. Melanie nudged open her own bedroom door. The mounds of dirty clothes and the scattered pages of unfinished homework completely covered her floor. On her bed her large cat, Stuffie, stared at her with glassy, unblinking eyes. Melanie backed away.

She left her mother's bedroom for last.

Either she was there, dead, or she was truly gone.

Biting her lip, both hands tightened into fists, Melanie prodded the door open with her foot.

It creaked almost gleefully.

Her mother's tattered housecoat was tossed diagonally across her bedspread. The sleeves outspread, Melanie could almost picture her mother's lifeless body.

A jagged sigh escaped from Melanie's lips.

Her mum had never left her alone before. Without saying a word. Ever.

Hot tears swelled in the back of Melanie's throat, but she swallowed hard and did not make a sound.

It's okay! she thought angrily. I'm fourteen after all! I'm not a baby.

Her classmates had always called her retarded. "Fat crow girl," they jeered and goaded, because crows always seemed to be nearby when Melanie was around. "Retard!" because Melanie still held her mother's hand when they went out together. Because she did so poorly in school, never said the expected things if she spoke at all.

Melanie dragged her forearm across her eyes. She knew it was wrong of them to call her that name.

Her mum wasn't well, had never been well, and needed her to be near. Sometimes her mother looked so faded it was like she could disappear. But if Melanie stayed close to her, stayed in physical contact, her mother's color grew brighter. Her icy hands would slowly warm.

How cold her mother must be, away in the growing darkness . . .

Melanie's downcast eyes fell upon the few framed photos on her mother's bed stand. Her mother hated having her photo taken, and there was only one of her and Melanie's father, together, before Melanie had been born. Melanie had pored over the image when she was younger.

In it her parents looked so frightened and odd. Melanie took after her father, with her round face and downward-tilted eyes. "Watermelon seed smile," her mum used to say.

The photo was sepia colored, as if it had been taken in the 1800s, and the image was grainy and fading. Her mum looked too young to be pregnant, and her father looked dazed and rather hopeless. Melanie shook her head. How could her mother be waiting for someone like him?

Melanie tilted her head to one side. She flipped the frame over and pried the cheap cardboard back. Slid out the contents.

It wasn't a real photo, it was a duplicate on a piece of paper, folded up to fit inside the frame. Melanie frowned. She slowly opened the folds. There was nothing written upon the back. She turned the sheet over.

It was a cheap reproduction of a "Wanted" poster, like the kind people posed for at carnivals and amusement parks.

Melanie read the details written below the image.

WANTED: *For having appallingly become with child and risking the Half Lives of all citizens of Half World. Fumiko and Shinobu Tamaki are considered pregnant and extremely dangerous. Last seen seeking passage into the Realm of Flesh. They must be caught and the pregnancy must be terminated. Under no circumstances must a child be born in Half World.*

All sightings are to be reported to Mr. Glueskin at the Mirages Hotel. Creatures found harboring the fugitives will be treated with perpetual cruelty—psychological, emotional, and physical.

Melanie felt sick.

Had her mother really felt this way? About her? Before she had her? What an awful, awful thing to joke about.

Why had her mother kept this? If it was true that she was unwanted, then obviously her father had just abandoned them. Her mother had had her after all, because of guilt or something, but she never really wanted to become a mother in the first place. . . .

And that was why she was gone now.

Melanie let the awful poster fall to the floor.

She ran out of the room and stood, breathing hard, in the middle of the hallway.

"No!"

Melanie's voice was so loud she startled herself.

"No," she said with quiet determination. Her mum had never said one cruel thing to her, ever! It had always been the two of them, together, against the hard and exhausting world.

The fridge was empty and there was nothing left to eat; that was why her mum had gone out in the evening. Maybe she went to Fujiya to salvage the boxed lunches they threw out at the end of the day. That was all. She had roused the energy to find them some dinner even though she had looked so ill this morning. Her mum would be back soon. Melanie would not think about the fortune cookie message. It had only been a weird coincidence.

She thrust her wet hand into her soaking coat pocket. It wasn't waterproof, and the cheap paper had disintegrated into grainy pieces.

She would wait for her mum in the living room, with all the lights on. She would watch TV underneath the blanket. As Melanie walked toward the TV, she saw the handset of the telephone on the dirty carpet. She frowned.

She glanced at the empty cradle, then raised the receiver to her ear. It was silent. She pressed the switch hook, once, twice, but there was no dial tone. Of course not. Their service had been terminated five months ago because of unpaid bills. Her mum must have knocked it off the cradle. Melanie returned the handset to its place and sat on the sagging couch.

Her eyes were pulled toward the pictures on the wall. Her mother had cut them out from old calendars and placed them into used frames Melanie had salvaged from recycling bins.

Her mum had such odd taste in art. Nightmare images of Frida Kahlo in a bathtub, her double row of toes reflected away from the crease of the waterline, looking less like feet and more like something fleshy that crawled out of the sea. In the bathwater a building erupted in the crater of a burning volcano, and a dead woman lay with string tied around her neck, insects traversing the taut thread. Her mum also loved Bosch's freakish idea of Hell, the helmet-headed chimeras and vulnerably naked people. A man whose arms were tree trunks, which ended in rowboats, his chest broken open like an eggshell, with people being tormented inside him. A bird-headed man gobbling a naked person, while he pooped out the others he'd already eaten. It was so gross and weird. Her least disturbing artist was Escher, but his strange up-and-down perspectives made Melanie's head spin with confusion if she tried to figure out how he made it work. Something quavery and hollow ballooned inside Melanie's chest.

She needed to fill up the room with noise, and to keep her mind off of troubling things.

Her mum would be home soon, with cold but delicious boxed lunches, Melanie decided. She pushed her dark, wet strands of hair behind her ears and wrapped her blanket around her like a cocoon. She clicked on the TV from beneath the covers. No, not a food program. It would be torture. No, not a documentary of humans being eaten by predators. No, not the news with its barrage of war, mass murders, missing children, and bludgeoned dogs. A rerun of an old science fiction series. Yes.

THREE

"—WHAT!"

She jerked bolt upright.

Where? Something was wrong—

An infomercial was demonstrating a chopper/dicer; otherwise, the house was silent. Melanie sagged back onto the couch.

Tock, tock, tock.

Melanie whipped her head around. The sound was coming from behind the closed curtain.

The clock on the wall read 3:58 A.M.

Was it her mum? At the window? Too weak to open the door? Or was it someone else....

Heart tripping, Melanie wrapped the blanket tightly around herself and crept softly to the window.

Please, she thought. Let there not be a strange face, pressed against the glass....

She pinched a corner of the stained cloth. She slowly pulled it away from the window.

For a moment she could not see anything except the reflection of her own pale, frightened face.

Movement. A glint of light.

It was a small black eye . . . A crow. A wet crow peered at her through the glass, its head tilted to one side. The crow winked. Opened wide its black beak to reveal its red maw. It made a strange popping sound, barely discernible through the window.

The phone rang.

Melanie shrieked.

She spun around, her heart pounding.

Only to be filled with elation.

Her mum! Her mum was calling to let her know where she was!

Melanie ran to the phone and snatched up the receiver. "Hello!" she cried eagerly. "Hello? Mummy?"

The line crackled loudly. Melanie thought she could hear a faint voice trying to break through the static.

"Hello!" Melanie shouted. "I can't hear you!"

Someone was talking. She was certain of it, but she could not distinguish the words. She could just catch the inflections of language. Melanie strained with all her might to hear what was being said.

A high-pitched whine suddenly turned into an electric scream. "Uh!" Melanie shouted, whipping the receiver away from her ear.

"Hullo. Hullo, there," a male voice said clearly.

Melanie desperately raised the receiver. "Yes! I can hear you!"

"How charming," the voice replied.

Melanie blinked doubtfully. The moist voice was unfamiliar. And somehow unpleasant . . .

The person, as if sensing Melanie's discomfort, took on a new tone. "You don't know me, but I know your mummy and daddy from waaaaaaaay, waaaaay back. I'm their old friend Mr. Glueskin." The voice was sticky with sweet insincerity.

"Where is she?" Melanie cried.

"Please!" the voice was indignant. "No need to shriek! I can hear you quite fine." The man began hacking, sucking up phlegm and clearing his throat. Melanie could hear a wet retching. A sticky splat.

"Excuse me," the overwet voice murmured. "Pardon me. I have slight congestion. Never mind. I'm calling about your mummy."

Melanie's arms prickled with a rush of goose bumps. Something was wrong. She didn't know what, but she could feel it all over. "Yes?" she quavered.

"Your mummy had an *obligation*. We had a deal. She gave her word, but she broke her promise. That wasn't very nice at all, was it?" The sticky voice laughed, like he was joking.

Melanie's hand shook. This was a prank call. He was a perv or something, and she shouldn't listen to him. He was bad. She slowly began to lower the receiver toward the cradle.

"Don't!" the voice roared.

Melanie, heart quaking, obeyed.

"Listen, you little half-wit," the stranger hissed. "Don't you dare hang up on me! Your parents made a deal. I let your mother have fourteen years with you in the Realm of Flesh, but when I said it was time you both had to return. Well, Mummy came back to Half World like she was told, but she thought she could leave you behind and I wouldn't be able to get to you. But if you don't come to Half World I'm going to hurt your mummy, aren't I? I'm going to make her scream, and I'll call you. Wherever you are. And you'll have to listen."

"Please," Melanie said hoarsely. She couldn't think. He was mad, obviously. But could he really have her mother?

"Of course I have her," the creepy voice replied conversationally. "Let me call her over." His voice dropped conspiratorially. "She hasn't been herself. Not that she was ever much to begin with. But if she was always half of what she was, maybe now she's a quarter." The sound of rustling.

"Fumiko!" He whistled encouragingly.

Melanie heard him calling her mother like she was a dog.

"C'mere! Come on! That's a good girl. Someone wants to talk to you. Here. Take the phone. That's it. Now say 'hello.'"

"Hello," a soft voice said.

Melanie's hand shook. "Mum?" she whispered. "Mummy, is that you?"

"Hello," the familiar voice repeated, in the exact same tone. "Hello."

"Say something else!" Melanie heard the sticky male voice command. "Say, 'Darling Melanie, come and save me.'"

"Darling Melanie, come and save me," her mother's monotone parroted.

Hope withered inside Melanie. It was true. A madman had her mother.

"Give it back," Melanie heard the grotesque man say. Something clacked and banged.

"No." Her mother's voice was weak. "Melanie. Stay awa—"

A loud thud.

Melanie's heart stopped.

"I guess there's a little life left in her yet," the repulsive voice chuckled. "Surprising ol' gal, she is. Where was I? Ahhh, yes. If you ever want to see your mummy again, and so on and so forth, leave the house immediately and proceed to the Cassiar Tunnel. Enter the tunnel that is farthest west. I really don't know where you'll end up if you go through the wrong Gate. So PAY ATTEN-TION!" he roared.

"West side," Melanie sobbed.

"Good girl," the vile voice soothed. "You'll find there are numerous doors lining the inside wall. Go through door number four! Get it? Door four! Your prize-winning entry into Half World!"

"P-please," Melanie quavered, "don't hurt her."

"*P-please, don't hurt her,*" he mimicked in a falsetto. His voice dropped low. "You better get your fat ass over here. You better start RUNNING!"

Melanie slammed the phone into the cradle. She looked frantically about the room. What should she do? Her mum was kidnapped! She needed help. Adult help. It was a trap. She couldn't go to the Cassiar Tunnel by herself. Her parents were caught up in some kind of criminal past. She should phone the police!

She grabbed the receiver once more and raised it to her ear.

There was no dial tone.

Melanie jabbed the switch hook, once, twice, three times.

Silence.

The phone was dead. He had cut the line. That hideous man had—

Melanie's eyes widened. The receiver fell from her nerveless fingers onto the carpet. She slowly backed away from the phone.

It shouldn't have rung. The phone shouldn't have worked.

Their service had been terminated five months ago....

Melanie's heart bulged into the back of her throat. She could scarcely hold back a wave of nausea, and when she closed her eyes white lights flared behind her eyelids. Instinctively she sank to her haunches and took slow, deep breaths. When the dizziness passed she stood up. Snatched her mother's overlarge khaki-colored industrial coat with the fake wool collar. She pulled it on, and for a moment the smell of her mum enfolded her. Melanie shook her head.

What else? What should she take with her?

She didn't know ... just go! Go!

She slammed the door shut.

The cold night wind pressed against her face with a wet touch.

From inside the house the phone began ringing once more.

Melanie ran.

◎

Her adrenaline burned off quickly, and soon all she could muster was a shuffling jog. The rain had turned into soft patters; her mother's coat was not soaked through, but she was very cold.

In the early hours of the morning, it all seemed so surreal. Maybe she had dreamt it all; maybe she was dreaming this very moment.

What if it was all a joke? Some kind of elaborate trick ... but who would do such a thing?

She came to a standstill, her breath escaping her lips in small puffs. Melanie looked up. She had stopped in front of Ms. Wei's corner market.

Ms. Wei . . . Ms. Wei knew troubles. Her lover, Nora Stein, had been killed in a burglary many years ago. It had been the talk of the neighborhood, although Ms. Wei had never brought it up herself on those days Melanie had run into the store, fleeing from the Valkyries. Ms. Wei had been sad for years but she had somehow survived her pain. There was something about the old woman. . . . She wasn't the type of person anyone would go to for a hug, but there was a kind of strength about her. Compassion. On rainy afternoons, Ms. Wei would beckon Melanie to come inside and give her a free hot chocolate. They chatted about books, the cleverness of crows, and why sometimes people turned into bullies. . . . Ms. Wei never pried, but she would give Melanie loaves of day-old bread and sometimes soy milk and eggs. At the very least, Melanie could tell her that she was going to the Cassiar Tunnel, so one person in the world would know if she disappeared from the face of the earth.

The sound of a window opening.

A round glare of light, blinding.

Melanie raised her arm to shield her eyes.

"Who's there?!" a strong voice demanded. "What do you think you're doing!"

"It's me," Melanie answered in a small voice.

"Is that Melanie?" Ms. Wei asked wonderingly. "At this time of night? Is she in trouble?"

Tears of relief and gratitude filled Melanie's eyes at the sound of concern in Ms. Wei's voice. She could not stop a jagged sob from escaping.

"Stay there!" Ms. Wei commanded. The glare of light clicked off and Melanie, suddenly blinded by its absence, heard a window slam shut. Shortly, the light above the store door was turned on and Ms. Wei was standing there, gesturing, *come, enter!* Melanie could not help smiling with relief. She ran inside.

The familiar smells of dried mushrooms and papayas, lemongrass and durian filled the warm air, and the horror of the night receded.

Ms. Wei did not hug. She patted Melanie's back as if something were stuck in her throat.

"Melanie is in trouble. Melanie needs help."

Melanie blinked through her tears, smiling. She loved how Ms. Wei always used the third person. She didn't know why, but it somehow made things seem slightly more manageable....

Ms. Wei did not wait for an answer she already knew. "Come! Come upstairs!"

She turned off the lights and they made their way up a narrow staircase at the back of the store.

Melanie had never been inside Ms. Wei's living space before.

Most of the floor had been opened up so that the living room and the kitchen were combined. The wide-open space was welcoming and airy. The north wall was completely lined with books, the titles on the spines written in Chinese, French, German, and English. Two tall metal filing cabinets, two comfortable-looking chairs, and a large reading lamp were placed near the window of the west wall. An enormous wooden table, covered with books, stacks of paper, and drawings, occupied the center of the floor. An orange tree filled one corner of the room, the leaves almost brushing against the high, sloped ceiling. Tiny fruit hung from the branches. The air smelled spicy with it.

"Ms. Wei doesn't often have guests," Ms. Wei apologized. She cleared off part of the table and gestured for Melanie to sit.

Melanie sat on the crushed velvet seat and curled her fingers over the carved wooden arms of the chair. Ms. Wei put water on to boil in the kitchen. Melanie sagged back in her seat and her eyes began to grow heavy with exhaustion. She jolted upright when Ms. Wei set down a teapot and two cups with a soft *thump*.

Ms. Wei's crinkly eyes narrowed. She poured out brown tea, a nutty aroma filling the air. Melanie drank the hot liquid gingerly. It was delicious.

Ms. Wei's eyes narrowed even more. "Is Melanie hungry?"

Melanie looked up from her cup. It took several seconds before the words sank in. She nodded.

"Melanie must first eat before she tells her story," Ms. Wei said emphatically.

"No, I have to hurry. My mum—"

"Melanie cannot think or make good choices if she is hungry. Eat first. Talk later!" Ms. Wei went back into the kitchen. She set something to whir and turn in the microwave. Melanie heard the *crack, crack* of eggshells, the sound of mixing. She slowly nodded off once more until the *thump, thump* of plates being set before her jolted her out of her stupor.

"Eat," Ms. Wei said.

Melanie fell to the simple meal of hot broth, stir-fried pea leaves, and scrambled eggs. Hot rice. Each bite was full of flavor, savory and nourishing, and Melanie could feel her unsettled emotions grounding, her wits returning. When she was finished, Ms. Wei added more water to the teapot. She refilled Melanie's cup, then focused her sharp eyes upon the girl's face.

"Talk."

She began slowly, at first, and when Ms. Wei did not interrupt with questions or ridicule, the words tumbled from Melanie's lips. She told her everything that had happened that afternoon and evening. "As I was running from the house," Melanie concluded, "the phone started ringing again. And it shouldn't have." Melanie shook her head. "'Half World,' he said. 'Realm of Flesh.' Could such a thing possibly be, Ms. Wei? He's just a crazy man and I should phone the police, right? 'Mr. Glueskin,' he said." Melanie shuddered at his repulsive name. "Is this all true?" She looked up from her empty cup. Ms. Wei's eyes were closed. Had she fallen asleep?

Ms. Wei stood up so quickly, her chair clattered on the hard wood floor. The old woman rushed from the table to her filing cabinets. Using a key she had on a chain around her neck, she unlocked one of the cabinets and began to slide open heavy drawers, rifling through folders. The smell of ancient dust filled the air. Melanie sneezed.

The old woman was swearing. She slammed shut the lowest drawer, relocked the cabinet, then turned to the second one and began rummaging once more. "Hah!" she shouted. "Ms. Wei knew it! It sounded familiar!"

"What? What!" Melanie demanded.

Ms. Wei held up an old file folder with great care. The old woman brought her prize to the table. She ran off to her kitchen and came back wearing white cotton gloves. Melanie frowned, bewildered.

"There is natural acid on hands, on the skin," Ms. Wei explained as she carefully opened the folder. "If they touch ancient things with their skin they can damage it." She looked up and winked. "Ms. Wei was an archivist before she came to this country," she said in a conspiratorial tone. "Ms. Wei comes from a long line of archivists and scholars. One day, many years ago, a younger Ms. Wei was looking for interesting books at Macleod's when she found a very old copy of the *Tibetan Book of the Dead*. It was an edition she had never seen before. She bought it and took it home and this little scrap of ancient paper fell out of it!"

She removed a small envelope from the folder and gently tipped a ragged fragment of yellow paper into her palm. On the surface was a wriggling script that Melanie could not identify. It didn't look at all like Chinese characters, but what did she know? Her throat was tight. "What does this have to do with my mum?" she whispered hoarsely.

"*Shhhht!*" Ms. Wei commanded. "Look. Look and listen. Listen with your entire spirit."

Melanie stared at the script, and as she traced the strange lines with her eyes her heart began to open like the petals of a flower.

The wriggling script began to move, to undulate and weave on the page, the faint black ink re-forming into letter, words:

> *So ends what should not be*
> *when a child is born*
> *impossibly*
> *in the nether Realm of Half World.*

Melanie stopped breathing. Her thoughts clicked like an old-fashioned clock. That vile Mr. Glueskin. On the phone. He said that her mother had made a pact. Fourteen years. So that she could raise Melanie in the Realm of Flesh.

And—

The photo of her parents. The "Wanted" poster description.

It had mentioned Half World, too....

"Ms. Wei," Melanie said grimly, "I have to go."

"What did Melanie see?" Ms. Wei asked.

Melanie glanced at the script, but it had reverted to its original unreadable form. She blinked with frustration. She couldn't remember things exactly, one of the reasons she did so poorly in school. "It said—it said something about the thing that shouldn't be stopping. When the impossible baby is born in Half World."

"Ohhhh," Ms. Wei breathed.

"Is that what you saw?" Melanie asked.

The old woman shook her head. "Ms. Wei saw something else. It changes for people, perhaps. Ms. Wei's message said, 'From the darkness comes a Half World child to be well tended.'"

Melanie gasped. "Is that me? Tonight?"

"It may be." Ms. Wei shrugged. "This must be part of a prophecy. But the prophecy must change all the time as life moves forward. The prophecy must be forced to change, but it also has the capacity to change the future. At least that is what Ms. Wei has come to understand...."

"Ms. Wei"—Melanie gulped—"are you human?"

Ms. Wei's small dark eyes widened.

Melanie held her breath. Had she insulted her only friend? Or had she discovered the secret of the monster who would now be forced to kill her?

The old woman began to laugh. "Ba! Ha! Ha! Ha! Haaaaaaah!" she bellowed, wiping tears from the corners of her eyes. "Ahhh, Melanie. Ms. Wei wishes she was not trapped being a human mortal, but that is all we have. Some of the most ancient books on these shelves speak of a time that might have been. When we were not trapped as mortals in a world of suffering and hardship. A time when all living things died and went to different Realms. Many of the religions, now, echo this sentiment. Heaven and Hell. Nirvana. Paradise. Purgatory. Ms. Wei does not believe in these things. But a better cycle than the one we live in now, Ms. Wei hopes for this with all her spirit."

Melanie shook her head, her mind already moving toward the trek to the Cassiar Tunnel.

Ms. Wei placed the ancient scrap of paper in the envelope and put it back into the file folder. She removed her white gloves and began bustling about the room, tossing items onto a chair: a black backpack, granola bars, matches, several black garbage bags, a pocketknife, a coil of rope, a bag of nuts and raisins. She ran downstairs and came back up carrying four small bottles of water.

"What are you doing?" Melanie asked.

"We need provisions. Where did Ms. Wei put that flashlight?"

When the old woman's use of "we" sank in, a warm smile lit up Melanie's somber face like a beacon.

Ms. Wei took another key from a clip on her trousers and opened a small wooden cabinet beside the bookshelf. "We need them now," she muttered. She unwrapped some objects bundled in faded red silk and set them upon the table.

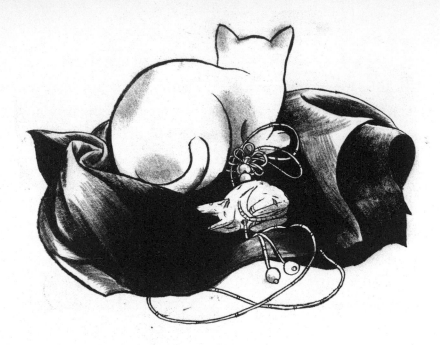

One was a small white stone sculpture. It was so worn with age the details were indistinct, but Melanie thought it might be a cat. The second item was a smaller piece of green jade, an amulet tied to red string. Melanie thought it looked like a rat. Ms. Wei held the amulet up to the light and it twirled slowly. The jade was a deep imperial green, darker in the center and more transparent at the edges. The old woman tied the red string around Melanie's neck and kissed her forehead as if bestowing a benediction.

"Let Jade Rat bring Melanie luck and strength. Jade Rat has been in Ms. Wei's family for more years than can be remembered. Ms. Wei gifts it to Melanie now. Carry hope and faith." The old woman turned to the small cat sculpture. "White Cat!" Ms. Wei commanded. "Don't let this old woman down!" She sniffed. "Cats are so self-centered," she grumbled beneath her breath.

"Now!" Ms. Wei said. "We are ready!"

FOUR

MS. WEI HAD the cab driver drop them off on the corner of Cassiar and Adanac streets.

Melanie stared wide-eyed all about her.

Adanac Street bisected the Tunnel from above. Melanie could feel the rumble of large trucks vibrating beneath her thin runners.

"Be careful!" the cabbie called out before driving away.

"Nice man," Ms. Wei muttered approvingly.

The sidewalk of the Adanac overpass was guarded only by a low double concrete wall. A strip of grass grew inside this barrier. There was nothing else. No mesh, no nets, no high fence. If someone fleeing along Adanac didn't know any better, they could hop right over the ledge only to plummet twenty-five feet straight down onto the freeway. If the fall didn't kill them, a vehicle roaring out of the mouth of the Cassiar Tunnel certainly would....

Melanie hopped awkwardly on top of the concrete wall and stood in the strip of grass. It was late. There were few vehicles. But when they rushed past, the noise and the lights were dizzying.

There was no access to the freeway along the west side of the tunnels, only a sheer drop-off, a concrete wall. But along the east side, a long sloping bed of ivy led to the freeway below. Orange street lamps cast a strange glow upon the foliage. In the darkness of the night, the green space looked almost sinister.

Melanie frowned. "How did you know we could get to the tunnels this way?" They were well out of their own neighborhood. How had the old woman known that this was the best spot? Doubt began to grow inside her chest.

Ms. Wei was silent for several seconds. Then she let out a self-deprecatory noise. "Ahhh, Melanie. Ms. Wei was very sad after Nora Stein was killed. Ms. Wei even thought she should just end it all. But Ms. Wei is scared of heights. Ms. Wei doesn't like water. So she thought she could jump off a lower bridge and get hit by a truck." The old woman dragged her arm over her eyes. She laughed. "But Ms. Wei thought it would not be nice to cause a driver so much trouble! So she looked over this bridge, then went home. Hah!" The old woman extended her hand so that Melanie could help her up onto the concrete wall.

They both stood on the ledge and looked over the side, at the roar of a delivery truck being swallowed by the tunnel.

"I'm glad you didn't jump," Melanie said in a low voice.

"Thank you," Ms. Wei answered. "Ms. Wei is glad, also."

They scrambled over the corner of the concrete divider into the sloping ivy. The mesh of vines wrapped around their feet and they fell several times before they were finally at the bottom, sweaty, scratched, and breathless. They stood beside the freeway.

The two holes of the Cassiar Tunnel yawned like open mouths.

Ms. Wei turned to the young girl. "The glue man. He said the Cassiar Tunnel. Inside the tunnel. There are two of them. Which one do we enter?"

Melanie bit her lip. Was it south? It had something to do with the sunny side. . . . "The west side!"

They would have to cross the oncoming traffic in order to get to the west tunnel.

The curve in the freeway made it impossible to know when the vehicles were approaching. And because it was a freeway the cars came so very quickly. It was like a game of Russian roulette. . . . After peering at the blind corner for several silent seconds, they clasped each other's hands and made a dash for the thin strip of concrete that divided the freeway.

A semitrailer roared by with a blast of horn. The vacuum of wind almost sucked them into the tunnel after it. Ms. Wei and Melanie grabbed hold of each other. "Careful," Ms. Wei murmured mostly to herself. "Careful."

They stood, shivering, in the middle of the freeway, staring down the mouth of the second tunnel, looking for the traffic that would come bellowing out. Melanie felt like her heart would burst.

The orange lights lining the roof of the tunnel were dirty with exhaust fumes. They could not see vehicles approaching. Melanie made a move to enter the Tunnel.

Ms. Wei grabbed Melanie's arm once more. "The glue man. He said to enter the fourth door, inside the Tunnel?"

Melanie nodded. She remembered it because it rhymed. "Door four."

Ms. Wei, who always looked like nothing would deter her, shook her head worriedly. "Four is unlucky," she muttered. "Four is dangerous. . . ."

"Why, Ms. Wei?" Melanie asked in a small voice.

"In Chinese and Japanese, four, *shi*, is the homonym for 'death.' . . ."

Melanie gulped. "Four means death?" she asked in a quavering voice.

Ms. Wei shook her head. "Homonyms are words that sound the same but have different meanings. But we avoid 'four' because of the way it sounds." Ms. Wei sighed. "We must be careful. It does not bode well."

They cautiously approached the opening of the west tunnel. Just as they were entering the mouth, a white car whipped past them down the feeder ramp and slammed on its brakes. The tires squealed and Melanie shrieked.

A blue and red light began to spin around them before the siren came on.

"The cops!" Ms. Wei hissed.

Melanie, hysterically, began to giggle.

A roar of a car engine accelerating backward. "Stop right there!" a male voice commanded.

Ms. Wei pushed the backpack at the young girl, and she desperately thrust her arms through the loops.

"Go!" Ms. Wei hissed. "Run!"

Melanie ran into the exhaust-filled tunnel, beneath the orange glare of overhead lights, the jade amulet bouncing against her chest, the heavy pack jostling against her spine.

"Halt!" the police officer demanded.

"Ahhhhhhhh."

Melanie could hear Ms. Wei's voice, but she didn't sound like she normally did. She sounded like she was confused and frightened. Melanie cast a quick glance over her shoulder.

The police officer had reached the old woman and she was

holding on to his arm with a grip far stronger than her voice.

"Police officer," Ms. Wei wheedled. "Old woman lost. Old woman lost!" She began to wail.

"You! Running down the tunnel! Stop!" The officer remained undeterred by Ms. Wei's performance. The sound of tussling. Melanie began to sob.

"Lucka, lucka, lucka," she gasped, her breath jagged in the filthy air. Melanie coughed and coughed as if she might spew her lungs from her chest. She ran along the raised walkway, toward the emergency exits that lined the inside of the wall. The arched doors were made of heavy wood and looked like something that would house large animals. What if, she thought, there were beasts behind each door?

She ran fearfully past the first door, for she could hear behind it a sound deeper and larger than the semitrailers that roared past her. She was running as fast as she could, but it felt like she covered hardly any ground. Melanie knew she should just keep going, but she couldn't stop herself. Sobbing for air, she glanced fearfully over her shoulder.

The police officer was forcing Ms. Wei into the back of his car. Her pale face glared at Melanie from the rear window. "Go!" she mouthed furiously.

Melanie began to sprint.

"Stop!" the cop bellowed down the tunnel. His voice echoed, resounded, and Melanie ran harder, passing DOOR TWO, which uncannily reeked of lily of the valley. The heavy wood seemed to emanate a sickly sigh, and Melanie held her ragged breath as she stumbled past.

She could hear the police officer's footfalls, much faster than hers, and drawing closer. Two late-night delivery trucks roared by, whipping grit into the air, snapping her hair wildly.

She wouldn't make it. He would catch her. He would take her to Child Services. Her mother would die.

Something slithered around Melanie's neck. She would have shrieked if she had the air, but all she could do was continue running.

Something clutched her hair and her ear. Something prickled with claws and whiskers.

"Don't give up, child," a small, hoarse voice whispered into her ear. "I will do what I can." A small weight leapt off her shoulder, and in a few seconds she heard the police officer bellow.

"Holy shit!" he shouted. "A rat!"

Melanie looked back.

The cop was leaping about, trying to use his nightstick to smack at the dangling animal that clung to his sleeve.

Melanie clamped her hand over her mouth. She watched in fascination and horror as the rodent leapt, scampered over the policeman's head, and scrabbled down his back. The rat looked up and glared at Melanie. In the strange light of the tunnel its eyes seemed to glow green. "Flee!" the rat screeched, before crawling around the other side of the officer's torso.

Melanie redoubled her efforts.

"This is your last w—" the officer started to bellow but ended in a scream as the rat clamped down on some tender part of his anatomy.

Melanie ran even faster. Her heart pounded in time with her feet. White stars burst in her vision. She could scarcely breathe.

She passed the door marked DOOR THREE, where a mound of clothes was humped against the wooden slats. She thought she saw an overblown hand, the skeletal remains of a foot....

The sharp report of a gun rang out, whining as it ricocheted. A second shot.

The tunnel seemed to pick up the outer waves of the sound, and the air began to vibrate, like the inside of a bell. The noise expanded exponentially, and Melanie was rocked by the force.

Then it was silent.

Melanie's steps slowed and finally pattered to a stop. The only sound in the tunnel was her tearing gasps for air, her shoulders heaving up and down with the effort.

All the tiny hairs along her spine stood up.

She looked back once more.

The entire tunnel was empty.

There was no cop. There was no rat. The circle of red and blue lights had stopped. The air was still.

It was as if she were the last person left on earth.

A car will pass, Melanie told herself, looking toward the opposite opening. A truck, something—the city never completely slept. There were always people....

The utter quiet was unbearable.

Melanie's legs gave out and she sank to her haunches. Her chin dropping to her chest, she covered her head with her arms.

Make it go away, she thought. Make it go away.

FIVE

A NOISE. IT was a familiar sound, but she didn't know where she'd heard it before.

Rolling. Like a bowling ball, but not so heavy. It stopped. Then resumed for several seconds before stopping once more.

The sound was coming from the opposite opening of the tunnel. The intermittent rolling was drawing nearer.

Melanie wearily raised her head.

At first she could not make sense of what she saw.

She blinked and blinked, rubbing a dirty, weary palm across her eyelids before it sank in.

The silhouette of a rotund animal pattered toward her, its rounded hump of body rocking a little from side to side. A raccoon. It was rolling something, zigzagging now and then, as the object sometimes seemed to go off to the side and stop. The animal chattered angrily when this happened, but it continued moving forward with great determination.

It took several minutes for the raccoon to reach Melanie's feet. The creature gave the round black ball a final annoyed push, and the object settled upon its flat bottom. There was a sound of slosh-

ing liquid, then it stilled. The raccoon chittered with great feeling. It rose upon its hind legs and clasped Melanie's jeans with a
small, clawed paw, very much like a hand. The animal's black eyes
glittered inside its dark mask.

"Is—" Melanie's voice was a hoarse croak. She swallowed and
tried again. "Is this for me?"

The raccoon vigorously nodded its head. It dropped to all fours
and began a rocking gallop back toward the entrance from where
it had come.

"Wait!" Melanie cried out, leaping to her feet. The echo of the
word lingered inside the cavern of the tunnel.

The raccoon loped away without a backward glance.

Melanie stared at the black ball. It was smaller than a bowling
ball, and it looked like it was made out of cheap plastic.

She glanced up and down the tunnel. It was still completely
empty and silent. She dropped back into a crouch and picked up
the strange gift, turning the orb around in her hands.

It was a large Magic 8 Ball toy. Black, the shiny luster was
rather pebbled from its long passage. Who knew where the raccoon had first found it? Melanie had seen one before, in grade
school. If you shook the ball while you asked a question, like
"Will I pass the social studies chapter test?" then held the ball
still, a message printed on an upside-down triangle would bob
to the window, where it could be read. It wasn't a real magic ball.
There were twenty answers and they were set. General answers,
like YES, DEFINITELY, ASK AGAIN LATER, and MY SOURCES SAY NO. A
classmate had brought one to school. After a few hours of asking
ridiculous questions like "Does Brandon love Kasumi?" everyone
got bored with the same old answers. Melanie had picked it up

last. She wrote down all of the twenty answers. Ten were of the "yes" variety, five were of the uncertain type, and five were negative. The ball, Melanie had decided, had very little potential.

"Don't be so sure," a small hoarse voice murmured.

Melanie gasped, dropping the Magic 8 Ball. It rolled until it came to rest beside a large green rat.

Melanie shuffled backward until she was pressed against the dirty tunnel wall. She looked about desperately for Ms. Wei, but the tunnel was empty except for her and the talking rat.

The green rat heaved a sigh and began scrubbing its paws over its ears, twisting back to groom through the fur on its hindquarters.

The red string tail looked vaguely familiar. . . . Melanie patted her chest with her hand, but the amulet was gone.

"You're the jade pendant Ms. Wei gave me!" Melanie actually pointed her finger at the green rat.

The rat turned to face her and smacked one finely formed paw against its forehead. "Aiyaaaaa!" the rat exclaimed. "Have your fears completely overwhelmed your wits?" Its whiskers were completely vertical with indignation.

"That's not nice," Melanie said reproachfully. "And of course I'm scared! Who wouldn't be?"

The rat sneezed so vehemently Melanie wondered if it wasn't some kind of rat curse.

"You're as big as a guinea pig," Melanie murmured wonderingly.

"I beg your pardon," the rat enunciated. "I'm Jade Rat and I'll have you know that I'm a rat in the prime of her life. Albeit," she added, "a life prolonged by stone."

"Holy crow!" Melanie breathed.

Jade Rat smacked her forehead once more. "There's no time to be ogling me like a creature in a circus! Haste, child! Go through the Gate! The tunnel will revert to its usual route at any moment! Aiyaaaaa!" The rat rudely crawled up Melanie's leg atop her jeans without asking for permission, muttering crossly as she climbed higher. "Why could not the old woman waken me when it is a time of plenty! With crispy noodles and juicy chicken and purple grapes and sweet potatoes? When the Realms are interconnected and the cycles in motion?" The rat sat upon Melanie's shoulder and slid its red string tail around her neck.

The tail was not cold and scaly as Melanie had imagined.

From a great distance they heard a low roar.

"Haste!" Jade Rat repeated. There was an almost inaudible click, and the rat was an amulet once more.

As Melanie turned toward the fourth door her foot knocked over the Magic 8 Ball. She stared at it for a moment. It was bulky, and she'd be foolish to take it. She couldn't even eat it. But that raccoon, she thought. It had rolled it down the length of the tunnel for a reason. Sighing, feeling slightly ridiculous, Melanie snatched up the dubious gift and deposited it in her knapsack.

She faced the fourth door. It was made of heavy wood and rigged on a single metal track, a simple drop latch keeping it locked. In the middle of the door was a big sign. CAUTION. ONCOMING TRAFFIC, it read.

What was on the other side?

Was the grotesque Mr. Glueskin who had kidnapped her mother waiting for her, a trap laid out to capture her the moment she stepped through?

What would he do to her?

Hands shaking, she pried the simple lock upward and grabbed the sticky latch. She pulled, but the door was stuck. She took a deep breath and grabbed with both hands and wrenched sideways. The heavy door groaned, the long unused pulleys shrieking as she forced it open.

Panting, she stared at the darkness.

Nothing.

Silence.

A vast roar ripped through the open Gateway, yanking Melanie off her feet and sucking her toward the darkness. She clung desperately to the handle as her body was raised horizontally off the ground by the howling, screaming wind. Empty cans zipped past her head, plastic bags, small branches, as tears whipped from her eyes. She squeezed her toes to keep her shoes on her feet. She couldn't breathe. The very air sucked from her lungs. Her feet and legs fluttering in the open abyss, as useless as a doll's.

Her sweaty fingers slipped.

Desperately she squeezed tighter. But her grip was growing numb.

She wouldn't make it. She wouldn't make it even into Half World.

Screw that! Screw the wind and the evil man and everything else standing in her way! Melanie pulled her legs with all her might, heaving with every muscle in her body.

The wind screamed fiercer as if sensing the girl's will. But Melanie redoubled her efforts, eyes squeezed shut, teeth clenched hard.

She inched her feet out of the opening. Slowly. Surely. Until her sneakers found purchase on something solid. The frame. Her toes squeezed hard as she started to pull the Gate shut. The wind screeched in dismay, desperate for its prize, and it seized Melanie's midriff, yanking her, U-shaped, her back arching, protesting, cracking. . . .

"Nooo!" Melanie screamed and heaved with all her might.

The Gate slid shut, and Melanie fell to the concrete.

She breathed shallowly, quickly, as her heart's pounding grew calmer.

"Holy crow," she muttered into the stinking cement. "Holy crow, nobody said anything about a wind." She patted her chest, and felt a wave of relief when her fingers fell upon the warm amulet still hanging from her neck.

"Ohhhh," Melanie groaned as she struggled to her hands and knees, tottered to her feet. She reached for the handle once more.

What could be next? A slavering monster? A desiccated human? Her school principal, Mrs. Nougat? Melanie almost managed to smile.

She needed to open the door to get to the other side.

Simple.

Unbearable.

Melanie wrenched the door open.

The air was silent.

She stepped through.

SIX

SHE STOOD ON a cliff ledge, hardly ten feet wide, hewn out of the side of a gray mountain. She looked up, above the open portal in the rock face, but could not see where the mountain peaked, if it ever did. High, high above her the almost vertical plane seemed to blend into a grayish white that was either cloud or sky. . . . When she looked over the ledge, it fell away so far, so deep that Melanie couldn't see the bottom, only small white pockets of mist. A cold wind whistled in fits and starts. Her heart and head spun, dizzy, imagining the horrific plunge, a deathly plummet that also called her, beckoning, compelling. . . .

She slowly backed away from the seductive edge, her heart trembling like a sparrow.

Something brittle snapped, crunched beneath her feet.

Little dry white sticks were scattered all over the cliff ledge, and they crumped into crumbs beneath her weight. Melanie raised one foot to stare at the remains underneath. It felt so disgusting.

A grinding sound came from behind her. Melanie spun around only to see the portal closing, as if an enormous boulder were being rolled in front of the opening. The circular passage was an ever-thinning crescent, until it was completely covered. The sudden silence was overloud, and the cliff face was a solid flat surface once more.

Melanie bit her lip. She could not go back that way.

And as if someone had turned on a switch, the air was filled with noise—the rasping, hoarse calls of thousands upon thousands of crows winging their way to their mountain home. Just like the ones she used to admire when she walked home from school. Had the crows been flying to Half World all along?

From far, far below, a glinting black thread seemed to rise slowly upward to where Melanie stood. As it drew closer, the erratic black line, undulating and unstable, began flying across the abyss as well as rising upward. The harsh rasping cries of the crows grew louder and louder as they flew nearer to Melanie, even as they stretched across the expanse of open air to a single mountaintop that had appeared three hundred feet away.

A black airborne bridge . . . They were crows.

Three feet wide, and bobbing and heaving like something tossed upon a stormy sea, the bridge of crows was the only way across the sky to the other side.

The sky around the mountain ledge where Melanie stood was blue, tinted with shades of sunset pink and lavender, but midway, the brilliant colors were leached. The mountain across the abyss was not vibrantly green with growing things but a dimmer hue. The sky behind it was slate gray. Everything looked flatter.

"The bridge draws near," a deep voice rumbled.

Melanie squeaked in surprise. She teetered on the edge, small dry branches snapping beneath her feet, and a large rough gray hand drew her back.

The hand belonged to a giant. Easily ten feet tall, her entire blocky body was of the same gray granite of the mountain. Without the sky behind her, she blended into the colors of the cliff face almost seamlessly.

Melanie's mouth fell open.

The giant stood still. She could so easily be a statue, Melanie thought. Unthinkingly, she stretched her hand to touch the giant's boulderlike knee.

It was solid, slightly cool. Stone.

Melanie jerked her hand away, blushing. How rude she had been! "Sorry," Melanie peeped humbly, looking up at the giant's implacable face.

She was staring across the abyss, her eyes the same matter and color as the rest of her body. "I am the Keeper of the Fourth Gate," the giant intoned, her voice a low, deep groan. "You must pay the toll in order to pass."

Melanie blinked. "Okay," she said in a small voice, thinking rapidly. "I have some things I can use to pay the toll. . . . " She started patting the pockets of her mother's industrial overcoat. There's bound to be loose change, she thought. I'm sure it will be enough. Because, she thought desperately, maybe the toll was symbolic. Maybe she just needed to make a show of some payment. She rummaged through deep pockets, rustling through old receipts and Kleenex. The crows cawed, their wings rushing like a fast river.

"Payment is the smallest finger of your hand."

Melanie blinked rapidly, confused.

"You must detach the smallest finger from your hand and offer it to me in payment," the giant said neutrally.

Melanie's heart stopped. "Wh-wh-what? You're going to cut off my pinkie?"

The giant was implacable. "You must bite it off yourself."

Melanie's heart thumped loudly in her ears. Small white lights speckled her vision. She shook her head, tears filling her eyes. "Please," she entreated. "Please. I can't do that. I have to get across. My mum . . . "

"You must pay the toll or turn away from the Gate. The bridge will wane soon, regardless." The giant crossed her arms with a creak and grind of thousands of tons of stone. She said nothing more.

Something burned in Melanie's chest. It twisted and writhed. Sobbing, Melanie stuck her pinkie into her mouth. She bit down at the base, hard, and she whimpered with the pain. But she could not bite through. She pulled her finger out and stared at the imprint of her teeth. She shoved her pinkie in her mouth again and bit harder, the sound of bone grinding. She wailed with pain. But she could not do it.

She could not do it.

"Stop," a small voice whispered sharply.

Jade Rat. Melanie hadn't even noticed the creature reanimated and perched upon her shoulder. Melanie clasped the animal to her chest and bawled.

"Stop that!" the green rat said fiercely.

Melanie flinched as if she had been slapped.

"You'll lose the bridge!" Jade Rat hissed. The small creature turned to the giantess. "I offer my finger as toll," the rat said clearly. The giant said nothing.

Before Melanie could do anything, the green rat clasped one

paw in the other and bit off her smallest digit with her hard, sharp teeth. Jade Rat spat the tiny pinkie at the giant's feet among the bleached, dry twigs.

"Jade Rat," Melanie whispered. Something cracked and snapped beneath her runners. She stared at the ground. And finally saw . . .

She wasn't standing upon dry branches but upon the brittle finger bones of the people, the creatures who had sought entry into Half World before her. . . .

"Do you accept this toll?" the green rat said hoarsely, panting.

The giant nodded. Once. Then gestured to the crows. Their raucous cries filled the skies and the flapping of their wings was thunderous. "Cross on the backs of the crows. They are a temporary living bridge between your Realm and Half World. Haste is necessary," she said evenly.

Melanie gasped at the open space that yawned beneath them. And the crows. Only a few moments ago they had been so numerous that they had made a solid black path, but now the path was starting to lose its density.

"Run!" Jade Rat hissed. Her claws clenched into Melanie's coat, her tail clinging around the girl's neck.

Melanie didn't think. She ran.

She leapt onto the path, her foot landing on the back of a flying crow. The smooth softness of sleek feathers. The oily slipperiness beneath her shoes. The flying bird sagged beneath her weight and just as it began to veer away Melanie leapt off, stepping down as the next crow flew in to take its place in the path. On and on, Melanie leapt. She could not run faster than the birds' flight. The bridge existed only beneath her and behind her. The crows flew in from behind to offer her feet a moment of surface. As soon as she set down her foot the trod bird was compelled to break its forward motion. It was a bridge that was perpetually falling away in front of her. If she stopped she'd tumble out of the sky. Melanie ran at full pelt, sobbing, gasping, as if each step were her last.

"Don't look back!" Jade Rat screeched. "Run faster!"

Melanie, told not to, couldn't help herself.

She looked back.

Only fifteen feet more of flying crow remained to act as a bridge and the mountain was still fifty feet away.

She would never make it.

"Move it!" Jade Rat screamed.

Melanie ran with everything she had. Five feet. Ten feet. Fifteen feet. She kept pace with the flying crows, leaping onto their backs as if she were jumping from stone to stone in a rushing river. . . . The crows began to separate; the bridge was starting to break. And Melanie could see the empty space between their flapping wings. I'm running across the sky! She was capable only of thinking, I'm running across the sky!

Only fifteen feet away. An outcropping of rock. Flat, like a landing pad, a dock. It was covered with coarse mountain grass and dark flowers. No colors. Only black and white. Shades of gray. She staggered toward it desperately. Her heart pounding close to bursting. Lungs tearing for oxygen.

Her right foot.

Empty air.

Eyes wide with terror. Mouth open in a silent scream.

Jade Rat.

She scrambled down Melanie's arm and leapt. Sailed through the air. She landed on a crow's back and sprang off, leaping quickly, lightly, from crow to crow, toward the mountain.

The rat did not look back.

After all, Melanie thought as she started a slow-motion plummet, she was a sinking ship.

Melanie closed her eyes as the wind began to roar.

Felt something beneath her foot.

The crows. The ones who had reached the mountain and had landed on their roosts, they had watched the girl's crossing. And for the first time in millennia, they flew back to aid someone who was meant to fall.

They streaked out in a dense column, splitting into two separate streams, looping around to serve as a living path beneath Melanie's steps. They were so many that the air was solid. And Melanie ran across the remaining distance with unspeakable gratitude.

She threw herself onto the mountain ledge and clung to the ground cover with her fingers and toes, her heart pounding wildly, heaving for breath, eyes tightly closed. Her head spun with delayed reaction. She lay there for a long time.

The scent of a sharp mountain herb penetrated her brain. She blinked blearily, and her eyes focused on a pair of scaly black claws.

The claws, sensing her gaze, clenched nervously then were still. Melanie raised her head. A large crow, head tilted to the side, peered at her with one bright black eye.

Melanie swallowed. "Thank you," she said hoarsely. "Thank you for coming back."

The crow stared into Melanie's face. It seemed to bob its head, then hopped to the edge of the outcropping and dropped away, wings outspread.

Melanie rolled onto her back.

The sky. It was not dusk, here. No sunset hues marked the skies. It was washed out, a glare of light that Melanie could not differentiate between clear or overcast.

She was in Half World. . . .

She sat up and gazed across the vista, toward the Gate she should have come from. But nothing was there, not even the other mountain. The wind keened with a cold voice in the empty expanse of sky.

How would she get back?

Maybe, she thought, maybe at dawn. When the crows went the other way . . .

She sighed. Plucked a strange two-petaled flower and raised it to her nose. She thought it might be blue . . . her hand. Though it was dirty and pale with cold, her skin stood out against the black-and-white hues of Half World, almost glowing with Life. Her jeans had taken on a dark cast and her mother's overcoat was dark gray.

"We must climb down the mountain," a small voice said.

Melanie looked down. Jade Rat sat on her haunches, her paws clasped together. Her imperial green hues looked closer to black in the light of Half World. She looked so dark her eyes were barely discernible.

Melanie blinked slowly. "You left me," she said, her voice catching in her throat.

Jade Rat did not look away. "You were going to fall. There

was nothing I could have done that would have helped you."

Intense feelings writhed inside Melanie's stomach. Jade Rat had bitten off her own finger when she couldn't do it herself. The rat had helped her twice already, even risking her life. But the rat's abandonment on the bridge of crows tasted bitter, bitter on her tongue. Melanie narrowed her eyes and clung fiercely to the wrong that had been done to her. "You deserted me," she repeated.

"Do you think you're the only one who has a task to undertake in Half World?" Jade Rat asked evenly.

"So you're using me," Melanie said woodenly.

Jade Rat just stared at the girl without blinking. Melanie saw that the rat was cupping one paw with the other.

"We must go down this mountain," Jade Rat said once more and turned to a small path that led to stairs cut into stone. The rat did not clamber up Melanie's arm to perch on her shoulder. The animal moved with a skipping hop, holding her front paw against her chest.

Melanie, following after, did not offer to carry her.

SEVEN

THE STAIRS HEWN into the mountainside were not treacherous, but each step was high, and after half an hour Melanie's thighs screamed in pain, ankles wobbling with exhaustion. And the heat from the colorless sun kept the stone steps unbearably hot. Melanie imagined that her aching feet were sizzling slabs of steak. Sweat streamed down her flushed face and stung her eyes despite the bite of cold air. They had stopped, after several hours, to rest and eat, but the break seemed only to add to their exhaustion. There was no end in sight and the afternoon glared mercilessly, the wind stinging, as they continued down the series of stone switchbacks.

Melanie had stopped talking to the rat. And the rat struggled silently. She had to scrabble from one step to the other, for they were almost twice her height, and her sides heaved with her jagged breath.

Melanie had looked back when she passed the rat. The rodent was practically dragging her injured paw, unable to keep it raised.

There's no blood, anyway, she told herself angrily. I've carried her the whole time until now! And my feet are sore, too. The exercise is probably good for her. Besides, she's made of stone. Stone can't feel pain. . . .

The excuses Melanie made for herself infuriated her.

She did not have it inside her to forgive the rat.

She glared at her surroundings. Half World. It looked like a clip from an old black-and-white movie. And what was "half" about it? It looked pretty much like her own world. Not that she'd ever gone hiking before, but this mountain could be anywhere on her earth.

They slowly descended from the mountaintop along switchback paths hewn into solid rock and sometimes stairs. The mountain terrain was dry, but sheltered pockets of rock held enough moisture and soil to support scrubby bushes and tiny colorless flowers. They were so very high that they could not see what vista lay below them. The light gray skies grew darker beneath them. Sometimes Melanie wondered if the mountain was also an island, surrounded by a slate-gray sea. Other times she was almost certain that a blanket layer of clouds was spread horizontally across the entire sky. There were no markers to gauge distance. And as they continued down, down, exhausted and wretched, she stopped caring.

It was if they were spiraling down the tallest mountain of all time.

As they slowly descended, the small pockets of plant life began to change. Sparse, twiggy ground cover grew into leafier shrubs, the flowers larger, a sweet scent in the air—but colors remained nonexistent, and Melanie had never known she valued them so much until they were gone.

And it was getting hotter. The hours of mountain switchbacks had them sweating and panting. Melanie thought bitterly about a school classmate, Lali Vukov. Field hockey captain and leader of the cross-country running team, Lali Vukov would have probably jogged down the mountain, Melanie thought. Probably whistling as she went.

Her mother's overcoat was ridiculous in the rising temperature, but she didn't want to have to carry it. She might need it later. Who knew how cold it became at night?

"Sweating like a pig!" Melanie muttered beneath her breath. She was hobbling down the stairs now, her knees wobbly, her thighs aching. "Bloody feet!" she cursed, limping, and stubbed her toenail on an outcrop of stone.

"I didn't ask you to bite off your pinkie!" Melanie shouted up the stairs. "Okay? I didn't ask you to do it!"

She sank down on a step, dropped her face into her grubby hands, and started bawling.

She had had enough. She didn't know how she would find her stupid and pathetic mother. Weak her entire life, only ever half there, and now stupid enough to be caught by a raving lunatic. Nightmare things happening. Ms. Wei probably sent to jail. And only an unreliable rat as a companion. How could she possibly save her mum? How could her mother have left her to cope with everything by herself? Her tears stung her burnt cheeks as she sobbed and sobbed.

When she was finally finished she wearily raised her head and dragged her coat sleeve over her face, sniffing loudly. Her eyelids were swollen and her skin felt tight.

She felt lighter.

The most oppressive weight of doubt and fear had somehow waned.

She turned her head slowly and saw Jade Rat sitting quietly beside her, her tail wrapped around her paws. The rat was staring straight ahead, whiskers bobbing in the cool mountain wind. Her usually bright and beadlike eyes were dull and dry.

She looked smaller. Less robust.

Melanie's heart shifted.

"Drink some water," Jade Rat said in a quiet voice.

Melanie nodded. She took off her pack and retrieved a water bottle. When she finished she poured some into her palm and held it out for her companion. The rat licked the water with her tiny soft tongue. It tickled.

"I would have thought your tongue would be rough. Like a cat's," Melanie said.

"The universe preserve us!" The rat sneezed with outrage.

Melanie smiled for a few seconds. She stared at her ragged sneakers.

She wanted to apologize for the terrible things she had said. The things she had said out of terror and exhaustion . . . but Jade Rat had left her to fall to her death. There was no logical reason Jade Rat should have stayed. Melanie knew that with her mind. But her heart could not forgive so easily.

Melanie said nothing.

The rodent set her tiny paw on Melanie's leg. "Perhaps it is time to try the raccoon's gift."

It took several seconds for Melanie to understand what she meant. Who knows, Melanie thought wearily. She could ask if she'd find her mum. The odds were in her favor to receive a "yes, definitely," and it would make her feel slightly better. . . . She returned the half-empty water bottle and retrieved the child's toy.

The black surface of the Magic 8 Ball felt slightly rough, as if it had been rubbed with sandpaper. Melanie frowned. As she moved it from one hand to the other she could feel the sloshing weight of the fluid inside.

Jade Rat sat neatly on her hindquarters, her small front paws clasped in front of her chest.

Melanie raised the 8 Ball to her ear and gave it a gentle shake. "Will we make it home all right?" she whispered. She turned the orb around, flat side up, to reveal the window. The *slosh, slosh* of liquid stilled, and a small triangle slowly bobbed upward.

CAN YOUR PART IN DESTINY BE FULFILLED WITHOUT YOUR KNOWLEDGE OF THE PART?

An icy breeze skittered down the collar of Melanie's jacket, and the hairs on her arms stood erect. She almost dropped the ball. Of all the answers she had seen in the toy, this triangle had never come up before. And her classmate's 8 Ball had only the set number of statements. Never a question. Melanie nervously cleared her throat. She wanted to leave the unsettling toy behind, there, on the stair.

"What did it say?" Jade Rat inquired.

Melanie reluctantly replaced the toy in the backpack. She did not respond for several seconds. "It must be broken. Or someone's kidding around." She forced herself to laugh.

The rat remained silent.

"The stupid ball said something about whether I can do what I need to do even if I don't know! Okay? And it's right! I don't know what I'm doing!" Melanie was standing, hands squeezed into tight fists, breathing hard and fast. It would be the easiest thing to do, to kick the rat off the mountain step, sending it flying out like a football before dropping for a long, long time. . . .

Jade Rat dropped onto all fours, drawing her red string tail around her feet. She looked very small. "I grow weary," she whispered hoarsely. "I will aid you as I am able." She seemed to shimmer. An audible click, and she was a pendant once more.

Melanie gazed upon the jade amulet. The Magic 8 Ball had asked her if she could do the job without knowing what the job was. How was she to know when the action she took was the deciding one? The one choice that would decide everything? She couldn't know, and every time she had to make a decision it would drive her mad!

Melanie grabbed two fistfuls of hair and squeezed hard. The pain was momentarily distracting. She unclenched her fingers and let her hands drop.

No—no, she did not want to become one of the kids who had to yank out hair, cut themselves in order to feel okay.

Think, Melanie told herself. But don't think too much, she admonished. Helplessly, she began to laugh. She took a long, shuddering breath, then let it all go. The most obvious thing she had to do was go down.

One step at a time.

She reached for the jade amulet. Ms. Wei had given it to her. For all that she was uncertain about Jade Rat's intentions, she trusted the old woman, and she would be disrespectful and wrong to leave the gift behind.

Melanie tucked the jade pendant into her mother's deep pocket, reshouldered her pack, and started descending the stairs once more.

She did not know how many hours she had been walking before she reached a layer of clouds. Suddenly she was knee-high in the gray damp of it. Dense, flat, it did not puff and roil like clouds in the skies at home. It was like a vast quilt spreading to the horizon.

Melanie could not see through the completely opaque layer. For all that she knew demons and winged monkeys crouched by her feet, chuckling, waiting for the best moment to trip her. Bite her. Gnaw her to the bone.

Yelping, Melanie scuttled up several steps so her entire body was above the unsettling divide.

What was below?

The image of one of her mother's Bosch paintings rose unbidden to her mind. It was a copy from one of the panels from *The Garden of Earthly Delights*. Hell . . .

With creatures and naked people being tortured, pigs wearing nuns' habits. Sawed-off ears and women skewered with harp strings. Why had her mum hung it up on the wall?

Melanie shook her head.

It must be so dark, beneath the layer of clouds. . . .

How much could a person endure?

Melanie took a shuddering breath and held it. She stepped down. Down, one step after the other, she descended through the obscuring grayness. For several seconds she could see noth-ing, and panic trembled inside her throat, threatened to burst out from her lungs. She did not want to breathe in the sickly clouds.

But she could not see.

She ran down several steps, then broke completely through.

For a moment she almost fell over backward because the stairs were wrong, she was going down, but when she looked at her feet the steps appeared to be going upward. She sat down, hard, her heartbeat pounding inside her eardrums, and desperately closed her eyes. It's only vertigo, she told herself. That's all. Because stairs that go down can't go up. It's impossible.

Except . . . except the Escher calendar prints beside the Bosch ones on the wall in their living room they had stairs going up and down, around and about, all in different directions.

"Oh, Mum," Melanie whispered.

Melanie kept her eyes closed, but she began scooting down-ward on her bottom. Like a little child she lowered her feet, then her bum, one step after the other. She continued this for a long time until the rough stone step was no longer. It felt smooth, flat, like tile instead of something hewn from a cliff.

Melanie opened her eyes.

The vista that lay before her was like something from a stranger's dream. A place of dark shadows, jumbled silhouettes of cities and jungles, forests and villages. The light that managed to penetrate the overwhelming layer of clouds created a shadowy world, absent of colors and vibrancy. It looked like early evening on a completely overcast day.

The city portions of the vista looked odd. Castle turrets

beside skyscrapers, pagodas and apartment blocks, tents and stone ruins, warehouse stores and freeways. The glint of light reflected off water, a nonsensical system of canals leading nowhere. Were those horse-drawn wagons? She thought they were horses . . . with scooters zipping past them, or motorbikes, tanks rolling with the grind of metal, the crumping of mortar.

It looked like every city and period in time were mashed together. Zeppelins drifted in the distant sky, and what looked like a flock of flamingos stretched toward a body of water.

Streetlights, gas lamps, candles began to bob in windows. Neon signs flickered, a searchlight spiraled the flat surface of the clouds and a siren began to wail. Bomb warning? Melanie wondered. She realized the flickering pale lights farther off must be fires. Things were burning. The air was smoky with it.

An unseen animal began to howl.

This was Half World.

Melanie's lower lip began to wobble. She slipped her shaking hand into the deep pocket of her mother's overcoat and fished for the amulet. When her fingers fell upon the smooth stone she clutched it tightly inside her fist.

"Jade Rat," her voice quavered. "I'm scared. . . . "

The stone remained stone.

Melanie's lips twisted. "Sorry," she whispered. She unclenched her fingers and raised both hands to push her stringy hair behind her ears.

As she navigated the stairs Melanie no longer had to scoot on her bottom. There was even a handrail, though she couldn't say when it had begun. She continued with her descent, anchoring herself with the railing, as she continued to gaze upon the frightening dreamscape.

As she neared the ground she could make out people; strangely shaped creatures dressed in human clothing; dogs endlessly chasing their own tails; a woman jumping into the canal, only to reappear on the worn paving stones to jump again anew.

A man sat on an ox-driven cart, a tangled heap of scrap metal filling the back. What looked like children chased after the metal collector. The children lobbed things at him, jeering and shrieking. The man didn't care. He was missing his head.

The roar of a jet sounded in the distance. Followed by a terrific explosion. The cloud cover throbbed momentarily with light.

The children on the street began to clap and cheer.

The spiral sound of a siren was overcome by the wild clanging of church bells, the distant heartbeat of an enormous drum, a deep melodic gong rippling across the night sky.

A flock of pigeons burst off a distant rooftop.

From somewhere a burst of machine-gun spray clattered metallic.

The stink of fried chicken, oily and rancid. Putrid garbage, raw sewage thrown onto the streets. Rotting offal.

A train on a raised railway roared past in a stutter of yellow rectangular lights, and was gone.

Melanie stopped.

She was no longer descending a mountain.

She stood upon the rooftop of a tall building.

The mountain stairway was no longer there. She anxiously searched for the place she had come from, crisscrossing the expanse of the enormous featureless rooftop, but the access to the mountain high above Half World had disappeared.

Maybe, Melanie's thoughts babbled, maybe it will come back again. After a time. Like the woman drowning on repeat. Maybe things skipped. And the stairs could come back in time.

Because it was the only way home that she knew.

When she turned around she could not stop herself from gasping.

Before her was a rooftop entrance, with walls and a door, where there had been none before.

Melanie stood there, heart pounding, until she was able to breathe again.

She curled her fingers around the jade amulet inside her pocket. "Lucka, lucka, lucka," she crooned as she opened the door.

She entered.

EIGHT

SHE SAT, PANTING, upon the third-from-last step from the
ground floor. As she had spiraled down, down the fire escape, she
had considered at each landing exiting through the door into a
hallway to take the damned elevator, but each time fear stopped
her. She ran into no one, but sometimes there were noises she
could not identify. So she had continued, soaked through with
sweat, legs so exhausted they had become numb.

Now what?

Now what?

She let her forehead fall into her dirty palms.

If only she were more clever. Like the smartest girl in her
school, Eleanor Cortes-Quan. They were both in the same grade,
but Eleanor had already skipped two years in a row, and she had
placed first in the provincial math competition. If Melanie were
smarter she could figure out what she should do; she could use her
head and make intelligent decisions.

Or if she couldn't be smart, if only she were stronger. Like
jogging-in-shorts-outside-even-in-the-middle-of-January Lali Vukov. Captain of the field hockey team and the cross-country

running team, she could out-bench-press all the boys and half the P.E. teachers.

What could she do? Melonball Tamaki, pudgy and stupid . . .

She groped for the jade amulet, hoping to touch the coarse fur of the rat, but all she could feel was stone. It felt colder than before. Letting the amulet fall from her shaking fingers, she turned to her last bit of hope.

The Magic 8 Ball felt a little different—the slosh of liquid that held the answers, the questions felt slower. More viscous. As if it were motor oil instead of water. Melanie clutched the orb in her lap. Don't let me down, she prayed. Please. I really need help.

She raised the ball to her ear and shook it gently. "What now?" she asked aloud.

Her voice sounded very small in the concrete stairwell.

She turned the 8 Ball over so she could peer into the window.

The triangle took ever so long to float to the surface.

IN TIMES OF CRISIS AND INDECISION WHO WILL ADVISE YOU?

Melanie hissed with frustration. The urge to throw the ball down the last three steps so it broke into pieces was a wall of red flames behind her eyes. Stupid, stupid raccoon! Why had it given her this useless thing? Maybe it was a trick. Meant to get her into trouble instead of help her! How was she to—

Melanie caught her breath.

The edges of the triangle were crumbly, as if they had been worn away . . . like the ball was beginning to decay. Melanie clutched the 8 Ball to her belly. Now that it was on the verge of disintegrating, it suddenly seemed precious. She had so few things left. Don't let this be lost, too.

No matter what, Melanie thought as she swallowed hard, the thing she had to do was clear. She had to find her mother. She had to bring her home. She replaced the plastic orb, reshouldered her pack, and stepped down to the landing. She turned the knob of the door, drawing against the heaviness to reveal a tiny crack, and held it open.

The noise assailed her first, the myriad scents rolling in immediately after.

It was a lobby of a hotel, but not like any hotel lobby she'd ever seen on television or in films. Across the enormous foyer, above the front desk, was a large banner: THE MIRAGES HOTEL. The sign looked as if it had been painted by students for a school dance.

The entire room was filled with the squawk of voices, loud, volatile, punctuated by raucous laughter. The shrieks of birds of prey, the hooting of lemurs, the jangle of coins and tooting horns. The rich aroma of cooking meat filled the air, and the enormous room was smoky with singed flesh and dripping fat. The acrid edge of burnt sugar, beer drying in the carpet, animal dung and cigarettes. Melanie felt simultaneously famished and nauseated.

The lobby was like a bazaar: a combination of a trade show and a market square. Businessmen with crocodile eyes slid payments of frogs and lizards into each other's pockets as if they were passing envelopes of money. A few finely dressed ladies had bird beaks instead of lips or reptilian tails trailing out behind their gowns. In little tents and booths merchants displayed their wares and shouted at potential customers, cajoling, begging, screaming for their patronage.

Sunglasses and thongs, flip-flops and wedges, silk scarves, razor blades, glass eyeballs, and skin grafts. Selections of breast implants were displayed on gleaming platters like rows of dead jellyfish on fun house mirrors. Dietary supplements were sold with promotional deep fryers and cotton candy machines. Rhino horns, tiger penises, knives, hourglasses, cuckoo clocks, helium-filled balloons, skewers of meat, candied ice, mini donuts, metronomes, rolls of lace, caged birds, snapping turtles, perfume or poison in small glass vials, and bottled water. Melanie stared, agog, with one eye through the crack in the doorway.

The wrongness wasn't just the freak show before her: there was no color.... Melanie closed her half-open mouth.

What she had thought were evening hues, the varying degrees of dark and light from her view atop the mountain, were also here, in the brightly lit lobby of the hotel. Everything looked like a black-and-white movie, Melanie thought. She didn't know if there was really color and only she couldn't see it because she was an outsider, or if it was colorless for everyone.

Melanie's heart caught in her throat.

She whipped up her free arm to stare at the skin of her hand.

In the dinginess of Half World her skin seemed to glow obscenely. Childishly, she thrust "the evidence" deep into the front pocket of her mother's coat. She bit her lip. What would she do? How would she walk around in this Realm? She might as well be wearing a neon sign around her neck!

"Oh, mercy me!" a wispy voice exclaimed, much too close to the door, and Melanie instinctively drew back as far as her arm would allow; to let the door click shut now would betray her presence.

"Vhat? Vhat?" a hoarse voice croaked.

"That Mr. Glueskin! He's so disruptive. I don't know why he can't just leave everyone alone to their cycles! I wish he lived at a different hotel! Look! That bellhop's going to get it!" The first voice, high and whispery, began to giggle.

"Not ghoot for bizness," the hoarse voice growled.

Melanie's heart stopped.

Mr. Glueskin here. In this very building! This was where he lived!

She drew closer to the tiny opening of the door. She had to see.

Two figures stood near her exit: a small girl-child, in three-inch heels and a bathing suit, a beauty pageant sash draped diagonally across her back, stood facing away from her, and a wallaby-like creature, with a man's head, was beside her, the tip of his tail flicking with agitation. Beyond them, in the middle of the sunken market lobby, was a wide circle of spectators. As they moved about nervously, vying for a better position, Melanie could catch snatches of the drama.

There was a loud *crack!* The crowd pressed back, away from the center, to create a wide space between them and the source of danger.

A tall, overly pale man, with tousled white hair, stood in the middle of the sunken lobby. His face was gaunt but his skin seemed to hang from his bones, as if it were too loose. He wore a plastic raincoat that ended high above his skinny knees, and his sticklike legs were ensconced in large black rubber boots.

Everyone was staring at what he would do next. The circle of spectators. The beauty pageant girl and the wallaby-man.

It could only be him. Mr. Glueskin . . .

Melanie resisted an overwhelming urge to giggle. Stop it! a sober part of her mind snapped. You're in great danger!

"So, where are you in your cycle?" the whispery girl breathed.

"Most likely sevhentee pah-cent!" the wallaby-man enunciated.

"Ooooh!" the beauty pageant girl sighed admiringly. "You've made it last so much longer than last time! And I love what you've done with your head!"

"Vhell, vhell." The wallaby shrugged, humbly but proudly. "Nothing laik you. You manage to ghet so maatch done before you ahhhre yanked back. Oh! Oh! Zehhhr he goze!"

Melanie looked across the sunken lobby just as something long and white stretched out, fast and elastic, like a chameleon's tongue.

Someone screamed, terrified. Hopeless.

Mr. Glueskin . . .

His tongue extended across several yards. And the white blobby tip—

It encased the entire top of a young bellhop's head.

Mr. Glueskin yanked back with his tongue. The boy squealed as he flew through the air, to land at Mr. Glueskin's feet.

Mr. Glueskin began to drop his jaw, wider, a great maw, his mouth hanging open to his chest.

"Ahhhhhhhh," the crowd of spectators sighed.

"So nasty," the little girl whined. "It's not like anyone needs to eat, here. What with their Half Lives. He just does it to terrorize all the half-wits!" She giggled and returned to their original conversation. "The beauty pageants have been soooo much fun!" she cooed. "I'm going to play beauty pageant lots of times before I try something else."

Mr. Glueskin was engulfing the bellhop, whole, like a python swallowing a pig.

"You are veree su-trong," the wallaby-man nodded. "But, you vhill come ghet me vhen I end ahhp at zee kiddee zoo, again, yes?"

The little girl turned her eyes away from the spectacle. When her profile came into view Melanie could scarcely stop herself from making a sound.

The child's nose was missing. A hole in the middle of her face, it was as if it had been chopped off with an axe. She placed her perfectly manicured hand upon her friend's furry shoulder. She gave him a reassuring pat.

"Of course I will, darling. I'll always come for you."

The wallaby-man dragged a small paw across his eye and cleared his throat. "Ahhh have alvays vondered," he coughed, changing the topic, "vhy, vhen you have so much su-trength. You do not feex your nohhhze."

"You're such a wallaby, still!" the child admonished, smacking his shoulder lightly, where she had been petting. "Isn't it obvious? It scares people. It keeps most of the bad men away."

"Ahhhhh." The wallaby-man nodded.

Mr. Glueskin's thin middle was bulging. He looked as if he were pregnant. His wet giggling rang in the sudden silence. He clutched his belly with two long arms. "Stop it!" he squealed. "That tickles!"

The chest area of his raincoat poked outward, once, twice, in different areas. As if something was trying to burst out.

Melanie, her hand covering her mouth to stop any sound, stared with horrified eyes.

The bellhop was still alive.

Mr. Glueskin began punching his own torso, hard. The squelching thuds were grotesque. And the entire time, he laughed gleefully like a boy.

The crowd of spectators began to politely applaud. Someone whistled. An overly eager voice sang out, "Encore!"

"I heard that Mr. Glueskin's organizing a party." The beauty queen child fluffed her hair with a hand that trembled. "I hope we're not invited. The last party took me an entire cycle to get over."

The wallaby-man tilted his head to one side, then the other. He raised his nose upward and sniffed the air. "Do you smell somezhing?"

The little girl punched her friend's arm, hard. "That's not nice," she hissed, her voice suddenly vicious. "And your stupid accent is reeking putrid!"

"No! No! There is truly a strange smell. . . . " The wallaby-man was turning his head around, toward the scarcely open door.

Heart quaking, Melanie began to close it shut. Just before it snicked into place she thought she caught a glimpse of a woman in a sparkly dress, approaching Mr. Glueskin. Her back was toward her, but there was something about the slope of her shoulders—

Click.

Melanie desperately held the knob in place with both hands

and fixed the side of her foot against the bottom of the door as someone tried to open it from the other side.

"I can't *smell* anything," the muffled voice of the girl said indignantly, "but I can sense something in the air. It's *intoxicating*!"

A snuffling sound at the bottom of the door. The wallaby-man was on all fours, his fleshy nose poking through the small crack.

"Ohhhhhh! Yehhhhsssss!" he moaned, snorting and sucking in great puffs of air.

The door began to buck in the frame.

"What is that?" The girl's voice was rising. She sounded high. "It reminds me of something. . . . I want it! Open the door! Force it!"

They were making too much noise. The people and creatures in the lobby would notice. They would burst through the door and find her. In all her living color!

The doorknob was still in her white-knuckled grip.

Melanie released it and raced down the stairs. Another way out, Melanie thought wildly. Hide. Hide!

"Through this door!"

The familiar voice rasped before she felt the prickle of coarse fur and whiskers against her face.

Melanie shrieked.

NINE

"Shut up!" Jade Rat hissed. "I can't smell anyone on the other side. But you'll draw attention if you're not quiet. Go!"

Melanie swallowed a sob and pushed on the door. It opened into the long empty hallway of the basement. She pressed her chin to her chest so that her clumpy hair obscured her face. She was never more grateful that her mess of hair was black. She thrust her betraying hands into the deep pockets and ran-walked down the flat floral-patterned carpet.

Jade Rat, hidden inside her hair, tugged her ear. "In here!" she said sharply.

Melanie veered into an empty women's changing room. She could smell chlorine in the air and hear the distant splash of water, a few echoey voices.

"What now?" Melanie gasped.

"Let me think," the rat said curtly, leaping onto the counter in front of the long mirror.

Melanie caught sight of herself. Her face, tear-streaked and red, her small eyes wide with fear and helplessness. She reared back, as if she had been slapped.

She turned toward the sinks. She splashed cold water on her face and the coolness felt good. Her eyes fell upon something by the neighboring faucet.

A tube of lipstick.

Lipstick.

Makeup.

Melanie spun around and began opening lockers. Empty, empty, empty. Jackpot!

A gray stretchy tracksuit. A towel and large makeup bag! Making sure that no one was coming through the pool entry door or the one leading to the hallway, Melanie took the items out of the locker and set them on a bench. She unzipped the bag. Jars of foundation, lipstick, eyeliner and eye shadow spilled out. There was even a pair of oversized sunglasses.

Yes!

She quickly undressed, thrusting her reeking, dirty clothes into an empty locker. She pulled on the gray tracksuit then ran her fingers through her knotty hair so it hung more evenly around her face. She grabbed a tube of liquid foundation and poured a large amount into her hand. It looked pale gray, the color of clay. She smeared it all over her face and neck, remembering her ears at the last minute. She slathered her hands, wrists, every inch of exposed skin. When she was done she looked in the mirror once more. She looked like a ghoul from a cheap horror movie. Melanie's mouth cracked open into a real smile.

The inside of her mouth looked luridly pink in the reflection. She quickly closed her lips. Dimly, she noticed Jade Rat nodding her head approvingly. Must not open my mouth too wide, Melanie thought. Don't forget. Don't open your mouth. Don't smile.

She rubbed eyeliner both above and below her eyes. Nice. She was looking more and more like someone from Half World. Never one to wear makeup, she overshot the edges of her lips with the lipstick, but it was perfect. She looked like she had applied it when she was drunk. Her lips looked almost black. She looked hideous. Lastly, she donned the sunglasses.

She was done. It was perfect. And she had thought of it herself.

"Good," Jade Rat said. Her voice sounded rather faint. Without its usual sharp edge.

"Are you going to sit on my shoulder or do you want to go inside a pocket?" Melanie asked softly.

"Pocket," Jade Rat managed before shivering back into an amulet.

Melanie, lips grim, unzipped a small pocket on the jacket and tucked the pendant inside. She did not zip it up, in case the rat needed to come out in a hurry.

How much life was left in Jade Rat she had no way of knowing.

Melanie's gaze dropped to her backpack. She didn't want to keep on carrying it about. She was out of food and water, anyway. The survival items Ms. Wei had packed weren't necessary in a hotel and the stupid Magic 8 Ball had done nothing to help her so far. In fact it was like an evil sibling, jeering, goading when she needed help the most.

Don't waste things, her mother's voice echoed inside her mind. *You don't know if you might need them later.* When her mum was between jobs and had enough strength she had gone out on recycling nights to look for empty bottles in people's bins. "Look how much money they were throwing away!" she would say wonderingly when she returned home, the cash in her hands.

Tears welled in Melanie's eyes. No! She mustn't cry! Her make-up! She blinked rapidly until she had control once more.

"Don't waste things," Melanie muttered. She emptied the survival items from the backpack and gently took out the Magic 8 Ball.

The entire plastic surface felt bumpy. The slide of liquid even heavier than before. Melanie took the towel and carefully wrapped the raccoon's gift, focusing desperately on not thinking in the form of a question. And returned the bundle and the remaining items into the backpack.

She slipped her arms through the straps. Glanced in the mirror one last time.

The tracksuit was good. She felt lighter. Soon she would be running as fast as Lali Vukov!

She smiled fiercely, with closed lips.

◉

Melanie discovered that her hallway was in the smaller wing of a T-shaped building when she came to the juncture. People were strolling about, and she could hear music seeping out of some rooms, the jangle of slot machines, and jubilant shrieks.

No one whipped around their heads to stare at her with suspicion. But she couldn't stand there, in the juncture, forever. She had to explore, to figure out the rules of Half World. She had to find out on which floor Mr. Glueskin lived, where he was holding her mother hostage.

Melanie turned into the main hallway. She kept her head low, so that her hair fell partially over her face. Her disguise was holding; she could only hope that her smell would be lost in the cigarette and cigar fumes heavy in the air.

Hotel and casino patrons jostled past her. It was both a relief and terrifying to be among others.

Her neck prickled with dread.

She could feel someone staring at her, from behind. She was certain. Her back felt heavy with the sensation, but she didn't dare turn around, to let them know she knew.

She picked up her pace, but the feeling didn't go away. A middle-aged couple was just turning into a casino, so Melanie slipped in behind them to lose the person who was following her in the crowd.

The barrage of the casino engulfed her. The blipping, dinging, buzzing of slot machines was punctuated by the screams of gamblers winning and losing money. Coins clattered on top of coins with a metallic roar. In the dimmer lights of the room it was difficult to make her way. She twisted right, then left, pretending she was looking at blackjack tables and games of craps.

Someone banged hard into her shoulder and she heard a tray of winnings spill onto the sticky floor. Melanie yelped with terror.

"Watch it!" the person snapped, stooping to gather up his hoard.

Melanie looked down and saw right through the back of the bald man's skull, a small round entry wound that expanded into a hole the size of a baseball.

"Sorry," Melanie whispered hoarsely.

She had to get out. It was unbearable.

She broke into a run, twining between people, and burst back out to the main hallway. Melanie ducked her chin into her chest and walked swiftly beside the wall.

Had she lost the thing that was tailing her? She wasn't sure.

A dark doorway seeped wisps of cigarette smoke and the sad notes of an alto sax.

A pale gray neon light glowed blocky capitalized fake Grecian letters.

AGAME NO'S. Melanie wondered what the missing letters were. The low murmur of voices coming from the room was quiet and almost soothing. She glanced over her shoulder, unable to stop herself. No one was staring at her, no one looked outwardly suspicious, but how could she be sure?

She ducked into the dark lounge.

Beneath the clouds of smoke Melanie could smell the sweetness of rum and the sharp antiseptic sting of vodka. Her mum had started out drinking hard liquor, but it was too expensive so she had switched to "healthier" beer. . . .

Vast rows of bottles glinted, lining the mirrored wall behind the bar counter. The bartender was as crisp and clean as a new one-hundred-dollar bill. He held his wares with a fine, cold grace, pouring liquid into glasses from bottles that never emptied.

Melanie slouched toward a dark corner with an empty curved booth seat, close to the exit. She could watch people as they entered and maybe figure out who it was that followed her.

A single candle flickered with a pale light on the round table. And peanuts! Salty peanuts in a bowl. Melanie's mouth watered. But was it safe to eat Half World food? Would it somehow trap her or make her sick?

Melanie looked around. It wasn't as if she could ask anyone. And she couldn't waste the question on the Magic 8 Ball. What if she had only one question left and she wasted it on peanuts?

Melanie slipped into the booth and sat down on the soft surface. She wondered if there was a legal drinking age in Half World. The alto sax twined around her, making her feel sleepy and sad. The place was three-quarters full, but most of the patrons were trapped in drunken stupors. Their heads lolled backward on the soft contours of the cushy booths and they snored loudly, snorting now and then for air as their larynxes collapsed.

"What'll you have, kid?" a tired voice rasped.

Melanie jerked with surprise.

The woman who leaned against her table looked hardly older than she was, but dark circles rimmed her eyes, blank and unseeing. A tray perched on one palm, the woman with the dead eyes and beehive hairdo had a tumor on her throat the size of Melanie's fist.

"Could I just have some water?" Melanie gulped. "Please?" she added.

The beehive woman didn't even answer. She wandered off, eyes staring sightlessly to one side.

"Trouble," Melanie muttered, slouching lower into her seat. "Bad trouble in this place." Hands shaking, she awkwardly slipped the backpack off her shoulders. She would try the 8 Ball again. Maybe this was the time it would give her an answer. Tell her where she should go next to find her mum. She had to get away from the Mirages Hotel. She wanted to find a safe place. Even in Half World there must be some place that was safe.

Melanie's eyes drifted back to the peanuts. Unable to stop herself, she selected one from the bowl and stared at it intensely. Would she be doomed to live out eternity in Half World for a single peanut? Her stomach writhed and growled with a deep gnawing hunger. She sniffed the nut. It smelled normal. Before she could change her mind Melanie popped it in her mouth.

It tasted like a regular peanut. The salt and fat made her want to swoon. Melanie had no more thoughts of enchanted food or fairy-tale traps. She grabbed a handful of the greasy snack and tossed it back. Keeping her eye on the exit, she continued eating with one hand as she awkwardly pulled at the zipper of the backpack with the other.

The first thing she noticed was the smell.

It was a heavy cloud that sank, settled around her in a wash of alcohol-sweet sweat, acrid cigarette smoke, and the putrid tang of dried puke. Slowly, unwillingly, she looked up.

A pale suit, outdated and too small, did little to hide an untucked dirty T-shirt. The man's beer belly flopped over the cinching of his belt, and his fly was down at half-mast. Flecks of old vomit had dried on the wide lapels of his suit where a crumpled tissue had been crammed into a buttonhole like a used carnation. Clinging to his arm was a beautiful woman with long black hair, wearing a floor-length black gown. Her eyes were completely rolled back in her head. Only the whites showed, gleaming, like peeled hard-boiled eggs.

The stinking body thumped onto the soft booth couch like a rotting corpse, the leather squeaking beneath its weight. It bobbled toward Melanie, unsteadily, and it opened its mouth. The wet sweet-sour breath of gin. The sweaty boozy smell was oozing from his very pores and the stink washed over Melanie's face.

"What'cha doing here alone, sweetheart?" the man leered. He slumped toward her, half falling, and his companion, despite her rolled-back eyes, grabbed his arm and pulled him upright.

"Thank you, thank you," he said, enunciating carefully and with great dignity. He turned to Melanie and blearily blinked his eyes. "You know, you kinda look like a girlfriend I used to have a long time ago," he slurred. "Can you take off your sunglasses? Are you staying in this hotel?"

Melanie cringed backward, shaking her head. Something felt horribly wrong. Something about him. She'd seen him somewhere before. In the lobby? Was he the one who had been following her?

"Cat got your tongue?" He nudged closer. "Come on," he wheedled. "Lemme see your eyes." He raised both arms slowly, his hands extended to grab her sunglasses.

His hands.

He was missing the pinkie of his left hand. The flesh wasn't healed over with scars. It was ragged and bloodless.

His pinkie—

Melanie stared at his face.

Her heart stuttered.

The photo. On her mother's bed stand.

She pressed her trembling hand over her mouth.

"You sick, sweetheart?" the drunk murmured sympathetically. "You can puke anywhere you want. No one cares."

This disgusting drunk was her father. . . .

She retched, chunks of peanuts burning sour and acrid, a mealy splat atop the table.

Her father nodded approvingly. "Better have another drink," he advised. "Before the last one wears off." He turned to his companion, who was waiting patiently beside the booth. "Let's take her to that penthouse party. You don't mind, do ya, hon?"

Melanie snatched her backpack and ran, ran, mindless. Sightless.

"Hey!" her father shouted from across the room.

She didn't look back. She burst out of the bar and into the light. A rough arm wrapped around Melanie's neck from behind, clamping a hand over her mouth, stopping her scream. The sudden grab yanked the feet from under her.

The attacker began dragging her backward. As Melanie tried to kick and scream, the hand over her mouth tightened and gave her a little shake, the sunglasses falling off, to clatter upon the ground.

"You have something of mine," a voice wheezed. "I can smell it!"

Melanie sagged with defeat.

She had been caught out. Her disguise wasn't enough.

The person who was dragging her was so wiry and strong. Her grip was like steel, and Melanie could not even dig her heels into the ground to slow their progress. The attacker kicked a small door open and yanked her through, dragging her down a long, cold, dark passage.

Melanie watched as she was pulled farther and farther from the light.

The small door swung shut.

TEN

SHE HAD BEEN caught. By one of Mr. Glueskin's denizens. Or a random mad Half Worlder. Whoever or whatever it was, she was discovered. It was over before she had even found her mother. It was all over.

The despair and fear were terrible. She was paralyzed. She hadn't even the strength to struggle. She was dragged like a sack of rice down the long, dark, and narrow hallway. The stink of mildew made the air thick.

The steely arm around her neck shifted.

The clanking of a heavy lock, the rattle of chains: it must be the dungeon, Melanie thought dully.

A second door creaked open. Warmer air wafted outward and brought with it a familiar smell, one that for the life of her, she could not place—

Dust and books . . . the musty and slightly mold-tinged odor of ancient books upon books. It smelled like Macleod's, where tomes were stacked into piles and mounds, riches mixed in with the pulp, towering to the ceiling.

The sudden glare of light blinded.

Melanie was dumped unceremoniously onto the floor. The heavy door creaked shut and locked with a loud clank. The vast room filled with books and scrolls and parchment and stone tablets seemed to lean in toward her.

Melanie stared up at her abductor.

She was an ancient woman, dressed in cast-off clothing, her scraggly white hair tangled and knotted, her small eyes glinting wildly in her dark wrinkled face. Her abductor was scarcely taller than she was, and Melanie quaked at how she had managed to drag her body so easily. Melanie took a deep breath.

"Why—" Her voice cracked. She swallowed hard and tried once more, her words soft but clear. "Why have you brought me here?"

The woman suddenly dropped onto all fours. She shoved her face into Melanie's and the girl scrambled backward, even as the old woman scuttled forward.

"Uh! Uh!" Melanie gasped, until her way was blocked by a mound of books.

"You have something of mine!" the ancient woman hissed, her face too close. "Give it back to me!"

My life, Melanie thought, her heart gulping inside her throat. She wants to be alive. Like I am. She wants my life for her own. . . .

The maddened woman reached out with two gnarled hands. But instead of wrapping them around her neck, the old woman began patting the outside of Melanie's clothes. As if she was looking for something. She found the unzipped pocket and eagerly crammed her hand inside.

The old woman gave a jubilant cry.

She yanked her hand out, fingers clenched into a fist, the red strings of the jade amulet dangling.

"Oh!" Melanie cried out, reaching out to grab the woman's arm, but she scurried back, holding the amulet to her chest, her second hand pressed protectively over her closed fist.

"It's here! Found! After all these years. These eons! This interminable Half Life! Jade Rat! Jade Rat! You are returned to me!" The old woman's voice broke apart. She sank to her knees, eyes closed, and great tears rolled down her wrinkled face.

From between the cracks of her fingers a green light began to glow, stronger, brighter, and the old woman opened her eyes. Wonderingly, she opened her hand and the brilliant light filled the cavernous room. As if a warm breeze was lifting off the small bright stone, the old woman's tangled hair began to stir. For a moment the air smelled sweet, like a stand of young aspens after a spring rain.

Melanie, her mouth slightly open, could only stare with wonder.

The green light flared, a halo around the old woman's torso, then it began to fade, growing dimmer, the rays shrinking, until all that was left was a small emerald ember inside the heart of the stone.

Melanie looked up at the old woman's face. The hard lines beside her mouth, the harsh glint to her eyes had faded. She looked human.

The old woman slumped to her bottom. She gazed at the glowing amulet in her palm. The face she raised was full of peace.

"Child," the old woman said, gently. "I thank you. With all my spirit."

Melanie gulped. Several seconds passed. "You're welcome," Melanie said softly, accepting the old woman's gratitude. She didn't know exactly what had happened, but it seemed that she wasn't going to die. Yet.

They both sagged with a weary sigh.

There was a shimmer of movement in the old woman's trembling palm. The small jade amulet shivered from stone to creature, and Jade Rat, stiff whiskers bobbing wildly with excitement, ran up the old woman's arm to nestle against her cheek.

Melanie's heart gave a pang of envy.

The woman raised her hand to gently cup the trembling rat. "By what grace are you here with me, after all these years, dear, dear companion?" Great tears rolled down the woman's cheeks. Tears of joy.

"Gao Zhen Xi," Jade Rat whispered with a softness Melanie had never heard before.

"I have been lost, in the mad cycles of Half World, for thousands upon thousands of years. And yet you have brought me light. I am like someone woken inside my own nightmare." The old woman shook her head slowly. "Child"—she turned to Melanie—"how is it that you have brought change to this place?"

Melanie shook her head. "I've come here, to Half World, to find my mother. She's been kidnapped by someone called Mr. Glueskin. I didn't know anything about Half World, but I think this is where my parents came from. My friend, Ms. Wei, she gave me Jade Rat for luck. She said she comes from a long line of scholars and archivists. . . . " She looked around at the immeasurable numbers of books in the cavernous room. The ceilings, where bare lightbulbs shone, were over twenty-five feet high and arched like catacombs. "Why do you know Jade Rat? Do you know Ms. Wei?"

"A long line of scholars and archivists, you say," Gao Zhen Xi repeated slowly.

Jade Rat, who had been lovingly grooming Gao Zhen Xi's straggly hair, pushed through the locks to stare at Melanie with one beady eye. "I was Gao Zhen Xi's pendant in the Realm of Flesh long, long, long before Ms. Wei was born. Gao Zhen Xi was studying transformations and transferring Spirit, in the tradition of foxes, just before she died. She placed some of her living spirit into the substance of my stone. It is only because I saw Gao Zhen Xi that I have remembered."

The old woman nodded. In her profile, Melanie could see something of Ms. Wei.

"I was an overcurious scholar in my youth. I dabbled with magic and alchemy and herbology." Gao Zhen Xi shook her head. "I wanted to see if I could leave a little Spirit inside stone. Because stone is inert. It did not breach the laws of the cycles. Jade Rat the animal was very old. I extended her mortal life but even I could not more than double her life span. I turned her into stone from which the amulet was carved. And when my death came upon me, sudden and terrible, I left a little of my Spirit inside the properties of stone."

Melanie stared at the old woman. She did not ask her how she died. It seemed too intensely private to ask for the details.

Gao Zhen Xi's head sagged wearily. "Upon my death I entered Half World, as all must enter. But before I could attain Spirit, the great division occurred. And I have been trapped here, in Half World, these millennia. As everyone has been trapped inside the Realm, since."

Jade Rat stroked the old woman's tangled white hair.

"Trapped how?" Melanie asked in a small voice. "Why did it happen?"

Gao Zhen Xi took a deep breath. "The Three Realms—the Realm of Spirit, the Realm of Flesh, and Half World—are meant to be connected. We should move from one to the other, in due time, as each individual lives, dies, half lives, then becomes Spirit. But someone or something divided the sacred cycle, dooming our Realms to an ungenerative deterioration. I don't know why! I don't know how! I only know that we are very close to complete disintegration. I have been studying long for the solution in my archives, but it is impossible to find the answer in unfinished books."

Jade Rat murmured comfortingly as she continued to comb her claws through Gao Zhen Xi's tangled hair.

Melanie frowned. "Jade Rat?" she asked. "Have you always been able to go between your stone form and animal form? Ever since then? Why didn't you tell me more about Half World if you already knew about the Three Realms?"

Jade Rat shook her head. "I had a slow and quiet awareness, but it was a stone's awareness. I could not act. But the Life inside you, Melanie, is, perhaps, special. You have brought change. You have returned me to my old companion." The rat's voice trembled with great feeling.

"That green light"—Gao Zhen Xi placed her palm upon her own chest almost wonderingly—"that was a little of my Spirit returning to me. And I am truly awake as I have never been before. Child, you cannot understand the endless repeating lives we must endure in this place. For eons upon eons we are caught in our Half

Lives, repeating our moment of greatest trauma. Over the years some of the stronger ones have managed to extend their patterns, and make small changes, and in this way we have built societies and cities, occupations and some kind of purpose. But always we are yanked back to the Spirit-breaking moment, to begin the cycle once more. Some have never been able to break their pattern. They die and return and die like we breathe in and out the air."

Melanie recalled the things she had seen as she had descended the mountain, the woman in the canal who leapt in only to reappear and leap again. Endlessly. For all time. Little children murdered. Women raped. Death and destruction in repeat for all eternity. Light speckled in her eyes, a roaring inside her ears. She weaved.

"Melanie, breathe," Jade Rat said sharply, sounding like her bossy self. "Slowly. Deeply."

Gao Zhen Xi rubbed her back. Melanie took slow breaths until her vision cleared.

Her parents . . . if they were truly from this nightmare place . . .

"How did my mother manage to break her pattern?" Melanie asked in a small voice.

"You must be mistaken." Gao Zhen Xi's eyes narrowed. "I cannot see how your mother could be of Half World. There is no true birth in Half World as there is no true death. Half World was an intermediary place where the troubled could work through their mortal suffering before becoming entirely Spirit and move on to the Realm of Spirit. After time, those of Spirit returned to Flesh. I can see no way for your mother to have become pregnant in Half World."

"But here I am," Melanie murmured. She stood up and began

to pace. She approached a large wooden table covered in papers and opened books, dust and pens. It looked an awful lot like Ms. Wei's worktable.

Melanie's eyes widened. "Ms. Wei! She had a piece of magic paper. It had words on it that talked about Half World. It said that if an impossible baby is born then it will stop the things that shouldn't be."

Gao Zhen Xi's small dark eyes narrowed. "Magic paper," she muttered. "Impossible baby? What could that mean?

"Wah!" she shouted, jumping upright. Jade Rat leapt from her shoulder to land atop the cluttered table.

Déjà vu washed over Melanie as she watched the old woman rifling through stacks of parchment, piles of books, as dust lifted into the air. Gao Zhen Xi scurried alongside the rows of books, her finger tracing the spines. Breathing hard, she came to a standstill. With shaking hands she pulled out an ancient tome.

Blackened with age, on the cover was a slightly embossed emblem. It looked like the yin-yang symbol, but instead of two pieces that nestled together there were three. Black, white, and gray spiraled into each other to form a perfect circle.

Gao Zhen Xi placed the tome on the table, saying nothing.

Melanie and Jade Rat drew close as the old woman began turning the pages.

"This is *The Book of the Realms*," Gao Zhen Xi said. "This book is unfinished, as are all of the books you will find here, in the Archives of Unfinished Books. There are far more incomplete books than there are completed, and they eventually arrive here through means I do not know. Words are Spirit, also, and when they are written down there is a power. I have been studying these books these long years to seek a remedy to the separating of the Realms. For centuries I studied its pages, but it is a prophetic book, and it was impossible to decipher. After a thousand years I could not bear looking at its frustrating cryptic sayings. But I remember. There was one section that spoke of a child born in Half World. Because this is an impossibility I believed that it was symbolic."

She carefully turned the almost transparent pages until she was two-thirds of the way through. "Ahhhh," she sighed. "It is still here. Sometimes"—she lowered her voice to a whisper—"the words have changed."

All three drew their faces closer to the page. On it a flowing script undulated like a strand of ribbon upon moving water.

Gao Zhen Xi chanted the words aloud.

A child is formed and leaves
unborn
a flight across the divide
When she returns
so ends what should
not be
a child is born
impossibly
in the nether Realm of Half World.

It was the last entry in the book. The rest remained unfinished, the pages empty.

The old woman clicked her tongue with frustration. "You see how vexing this prophecy is! How can a child be formed and leave unborn, then be born once more!"

Jade Rat did not respond. She was stroking her whiskers thoughtfully with both paws. Melanie's eyes caught sight of the torn place where she had bitten off her tiny digit to pay the Gatekeeper for their passage across.

Pay for their passage across . . .

A warm light seemed to expand inside Melanie's mind. "Maybe," she said slowly, "maybe it means two different children."

Gao Zhen Xi whipped her face upward to stare with burning intensity into Melanie's eyes.

Melanie flushed. Had she said something extremely stupid or offensive? Who was she to tell the ancient scholar what the words might mean, when she'd been studying the texts for thousands of years!

But Melanie could not shake off the *rightness* of what she felt. As if a puzzle piece had clicked into the deciding position.

"Go on," the old woman said hoarsely.

Jade Rat sat upright, paws held close to her chest, as she listened intently.

To me! Melanie thought wonderingly. They were waiting to hear her ideas!

"My mum had a photo on her nightstand," Melanie said awkwardly. Eagerly. "But it wasn't really a photo; it was a 'Wanted' poster. I thought it was a joke, but it said that my parents were wanted in Half World for having become pregnant. That the baby should be aborted. I grew up in my world with my mum. But how could my mum have made up a poster like that, if she wasn't a part of Half World? She must have come from here. And if she did, I must be that first child."

Jade Rat sneezed with frustration. "It is possible that you

are the first child, but then who or what is the second?"

Melanie shrugged helplessly. "How can I be born a second time? It can't happen. So someone else has to be born." A sense of dread began to grow inside Melanie's gut. No! No! Her mother would not become pregnant with another child . . . because whose would it be? . . .

Gao Zhen Xi had begun muttering something midway through Jade Rat's words. Melanie and the rat turned toward her and caught the tail end of what she said.

"—poster! 'Wanted' poster! Hah!"

She ran to a wall covered in square cubbyholes, filled to over-flowing with odds and ends, tiny bones, dice, tacks, boxes of matches, rolled-up parchments, and slips of paper. She pawed through them, scattering the contents upon the floor. She caught sight of something much too high for her to reach. Jade Rat scrambled lightly upward like she was climbing a ladder and retrieved the rolled-up gray sheet of paper that was tied with a bit of string. She carried it in her mouth like a dog. She deposited it in Gao Zhen Xi's hands, and the old woman unrolled the dirty sheet with shaking fingers.

A grainy image of a younger Fumiko and Shinobu. The lost look in her father's eyes. Her mother, pregnant, looking young and fearful.

It was the same poster that her mother had kept all this time. In the frame on her bed stand.

Melanie felt herself tearing up with a surge of mixed emotions, and her eyes glittered.

Her mum. She had done everything she could to protect her daughter.

She had been sick and weak her entire life, because she was never truly alive. . . . She had left her behind, and returned to Half World, in order that Melanie might have a life.

"Alive," Gao Zhen Xi crooned. "You are alive in a Realm that is not alive; that is why you create change. That is why you are capable of breaking the patterns."

Melanie raised her chin. Her gaze was steady. "If this is true, then I am going to save my mother."

"Is it possible?" the old woman muttered to herself. "Can this child hold the key to reuniting the divided Realms?"

"Perhaps," Jade Rat murmured.

"If only we had guidance." Gao Zhen Xi shut *The Book of the Realms*. "Histories will only account for what has transpired. Prophecies only recount what may be. But what we need is a guidebook! Something that provides direction! Bah! I am so tired I cannot think."

Directions—

The Magic 8 Ball! Its cryptic questions had meant nothing to Melanie, but maybe the learned old woman could shake some meaning out of it!

Melanie ran back to the pile of books where she had dropped her backpack. She carefully unwrapped the raccoon's gift and cupped the toy in her hands.

The old plastic seemed even more pocked and wretched than before. The surface looked as if it had been chewed by termites, and the slosh of liquid was slow and heavy, like a bucket of watery sand.

Melanie bit her lip. Help me now, she pleaded inside her mind. Be of use. We need direction. "This was a gift from a raccoon in my Realm," Melanie explained. "It provides messages in the form of questions. I never know what they mean, but maybe you will understand."

"I do not know, child," Gao Zhen Xi answered. "Let us try your orb of power to see what it will ask."

Melanie closed her eyes thoughtfully. The 8 Ball responded to the questions she asked. Could it be that the 8 Ball was not giving unhelpful questions, but that there was something wrong with what she asked? Maybe she wasn't asking the right questions . . . Until now, she'd been asking questions on the fly, all about what worried her the most. But maybe she had to think more widely.

It wasn't all about her and her mother.

There was so much more at stake.

Melanie took a deep, steadying breath and ever so gently shook the fragile ball. "What must we do to bring balance to the Realms once more?" she asked in a clear, strong voice.

She turned the little window toward her and waited patiently.

It took ever so long for a response to begin floating to the surface. It was scarcely a triangle at all, the edges were so worn down. The writing on it was so faded that she could hardly make out the fine print. Finally she read the message aloud:

WHAT YOUR
ENEMIES INFLICT
UPON YOU
WILL YOU INFLICT
IN RETURN?

Gao Zhen Xi looked thoughtful. "The response is opaque. It is something to consider, but I know not its direct meaning. Do you understand the question, child?"

Melanie, sighing, shook her head. It would not help them immediately. But maybe it was something that would help her later. . . .

A flicker of shadow swung from the ceiling and Melanie caught it with the edges of her vision. She looked up.

One of the bare lightbulbs was oddly distended, hanging low and swinging back and forth as it drooped lower and lower. Like it was somehow melting. And growing.

Gao Zhen Xi and Jade Rat looked upward.

As if sensing that it had been discovered, the white blob began pouring through the small opening in the ceiling. Like liquid plastic it bulged and rippled, cascading down itself, stretching long and gluey. The bulbous tip began to grow, growing fuller, larger, bringing shape to the smoothness, the beginnings of a mouth.

A white tongue.

It whipped out blindly and struck down a mountain of books.

"Child!" Gao Zhen Xi shouted. "Here!" She pulled a key from a fold in her clothing and tossed it to Melanie. She caught it with one hand.

The tongue, furious, began whipping randomly about the room. It zinged past Melanie's head close enough to stir her hair. She crouched low and crawled beneath the long table, the 8 Ball held in the curve of one arm.

"I found you!" Mr. Glueskin's sticky gloating voice rang out. "Don't you miss your mommy? Mommy's been asking about her sweet little girl! She's been crying out your name. 'Melanie! Oh, Melanie!'" He mimicked her mother's voice perfectly.

A snapping, whipping sound.

Jade Rat squealed.

No! Melanie crawled out from the protection of the table in time to see Jade Rat being pulled back toward Mr. Glueskin's melty mouth. His eyes re-formed, white with strangely shaped black pupils, he caught sight of Melanie and broke into a loose smile.

Gao Zhen Xi threw a heavy book at Mr. Glueskin's head. It struck with a splat, adhered for several seconds before sliding off. His head, flattened, looked so comical Melanie fought off the urge to giggle hysterically.

His eyes were enraged.

"Run!" Gao Zhen Xi commanded. "You must not die. We aren't able to die in Half World. Save us all by living!"

After a moment's hesitation, Melanie dashed for the door, the key digging inside her palm. Her hand shook as she tried to fit the teeth into the great lock.

She did not look back as Mr. Glueskin roared, Jade Rat screamed, and the heavy books fell with great thuds.

She grimly ran down the long dark passage. "They cannot die," she reminded herself. "They cannot die."

Their curse, this time, was a blessing.

ELEVEN

Melanie walked briskly toward the employees' wing of the basement. She remembered passing it before, and she had an idea if not a plan. She would dress up like a cleaning lady, for a disguise, and go look for Mr. Glueskin's room.

It was not much of a plan; she knew that. In television shows and novels the heroes always had an amazing way to fight their enemies. They made elaborate traps out of ropes and twigs or built bombs out of baking soda and batteries. They apprenticed with a witch or a sorcerer and developed their special powers.

All Melanie had was herself.

No, she corrected. She had allies here, and back home. Gao Zhen Xi and Jade Rat were on her side. Ms. Wei was her friend, too. Her mother.

Melanie thought about the torn place on her father's hand.

He was an ally, too.

And maybe Melanie didn't have any special magical skills, but she had the power to make choices. She was alive in a place that was not. She was not caught in the eternal loop of suffering and resuffering the same trauma like everyone else in this Realm.

Gao Zhen Xi had said that was why she was capable of making changes.

To be able to bring change into a fixed world, Melanie thought. There is power in that. . . .

Melanie found the door marked EMPLOYEES ONLY—STAFF RESIDENCES. She quietly slipped through.

The dorm was mostly empty. A few women and girls were either sitting listlessly on their cots or watching a television set up in the far corner of the room. They did not take notice of Melanie at all, trapped in a stupor of their repeat Half Life.

A young woman, not much older than Melanie, was picking at the stitches in her arm. Her dark raw scar ran from her wrist to the inside of her elbow.

Melanie fought the urge to tell her to stop. She cannot die, she reminded herself furiously. She will just repeat this over and over again. It was horrific.

This had to stop.

Melanie angrily began opening lockers. No one cared or noticed.

After several tries she found one that contained a cleaner's uniform. It looked like it would fit. She grabbed the clothing and went into the dorm bathroom. Melanie could hear the sound of deep retching coming from one of the stalls.

She ducked into a changing room and closed the door. The room had a long mirror, and someone had left her toiletries, a curling iron, and a blow dryer on the ledge. A small sample vial of a perfume called Poison. Melanie set the 8 Ball on the counter and unzipped the large makeup bag. Inside were scissors, tubes and jars of makeup, pencil liners, and shadow. Melanie quickly changed into the nondescript uniform. Her name badge, she saw, said GLADYS.

"Gladys, Gladys, Gladys, Gladys," she muttered beneath her breath so that she would remember. She turned on the curling iron and while it heated she brushed out her hair, all one length, so it fell in front of her face. She cut bangs so the bottom of the fringe came down to the middle of her nose. The bangs would obscure most of her eyes, but she should be able to see between strands of hair. She slathered on a new layer of makeup, reapplying the clay-colored foundation over every inch of exposed skin. She sprayed herself with Poison. She coughed at the sickly sweet stench, but it would serve its purpose. No one could possibly smell her Life underneath the vapors of a perfume so stinking! Curling iron hot, Melanie attempted to style her hair for the first time in her life.

She didn't know which way to twirl the rod, so she ended up with odd kinks and cowlicks, as well as sausage-roll curls. It looked awful, but it was also perfect. She didn't look like a teenaged girl; she looked like a frumpy middle-aged mother.

Melanie smiled sadly.

Would she look like this when she grew older?

If she even made it?

Melanie shook her head and stood tall. "Gladys," she said again. "My name is Gladys." Her eyes fell upon the fragile 8 Ball. It was beginning to look cratered and dry, like the surface of the moon. How much longer would it last? How many questions could she ask it before it fell apart? Every time she looked it was more wretched than before. Should she ask one more question, now, before it fell apart? Or were the questions themselves aging the orb so quickly?

Now, or later? Melanie waffled. Now, or later? She reached out to the ball, and when her fingertips touched the plastic surface it gave a tired *pop*, a zigzag crack spreading around the circumference. Melanie gasped and leapt back. Fine lines spread outward from the fissure until the desiccated pieces fell apart, like ancient pottery, releasing a mound of sand with a dry *hissssssssssss*.

Dismay filled Melanie's heart. She didn't know if she wanted to laugh or cry. Such a stupid, stupid way to use up the last question. There was no way she could put it back together again. Her last gift was now completely useless. Melanie angrily grabbed two handfuls of sand.

"Uhhhhh!" she exclaimed with frustration, flinging the sand down before grabbing two more fistfuls . . . when she felt a flat hard something. Melanie's rage faded as she slowly brushed aside sand to reveal a corner of plastic.

One more. One last question.

Carefully clasping it between her thumb and forefinger, she gently pulled it out.

The flat piece of plastic was rectangular, not triangular. The size of a bank card, it even had a black magnetic strip.

Melanie frowned. Was it a bank card? She flipped it over and saw the ornate script of the Mirages Hotel.

Melanie's eyes widened.

She'd never used one before, but she watched TV. Fancy hotels didn't use keys anymore. They had key cards you swiped like at the bank machines.

The Magic 8 Ball had given her the final key . . . the key to find Mr. Glueskin!

"Thank you!" Melanie said fiercely. She turned the card over in her hands. But there was nothing else written upon it except the name of the hotel. Her heart sank. How would she find out which room Mr. Glueskin stayed in? How many rooms were in this hotel?

Melanie grimly pinched her lips. She would find it if she had to go to every door in the entire building.

A cleaning cart! If she had a cleaning cart she would have a legitimate reason to be trying different doors! Melanie slipped the key card into the pocket beneath her name badge pinned onto the uniform.

The cleaning cart she found was heavy and awkward, one wheel having the tendency to stick, and she pushed it awkwardly down the hall toward the elevator. The cart creaked overloud and Melanie wondered if it should be abandoned. Head downward, bangs sweeping the tip of her nose, she could not see if anyone else was around her. It was both comforting and terrifying.

She almost ran into one of the two elevator doors before she realized. Unable to help herself she gave a nervous giggle.

Hand almost steady, she pushed the button. As she waited for the car to reach her she decided she would work from the lowest floor of rooms and make her way upward. She got into the elevator and was waiting for the doors to shut when a sweet young voice called from down the hallway.

"Wait for me!"

Melanie peered from between her bangs.

A room service boy, a silver tray loaded with covered plates of food held high above his head, raised his chin in greeting and expertly entered the elevator. His black trousers and white shirt were immaculate, but his black hair was clumpy, stuck with clots of white.

"Could you please press the fourth floor?" he asked courteously.

Melanie blinked and blinked. The boy—he was the same one Mr. Glueskin had eaten in the lobby of the hotel. It felt like a million years ago.

"Eh-hem," the room service boy said, a trifle impatiently. "Uhhhh, Gladys, is it? Please press the fourth floor. Four. Four!"

Melanie broke out of her paralysis and awkwardly poked the button. The number four lit up in the panel and the car slowly began to rise.

The young man glanced at the panel, then frowned. "Which floor are you going to?"

Melanie gulped. If she spoke would her breath reveal her living odor?

She released her white-knuckled clasp of the cleaning cart and scrabbled for the key card, holding it up as if to prove her legitimacy.

"Gladys," the young man enunciated slowly, "you have to swipe that. It's for the penthouse level." He sighed dramatically. "Dimwit!" he hissed. His tone changed, conspiratorial and mean. "I heard in the kitchens that Mr. Glueskin is organizing a party. He's ordered canapés and a blood fondue!" The room service boy leaned slightly toward Melanie and whispered theatrically, "He's in a foul mood. Don't I know it! Be careful you don't catch his eye!"

The elevator bell tinged tastefully for the fourth floor and stopped.

Door four, Melanie thought. The number triggered warning signals in the nape of her neck.

The silent doors slid smoothly open. The fourth level—

A deluge of noise smashed into the cavity of the elevator. Melanie clamped her hands over her ears, but the sounds of hooting, shouting, a high metallic shrieking stabbed into her eardrums. The piercing screams of a person being tortured. A deep, low pounding came from the walls as if someone were trying to break through. And a wheezy whining breathed in and out, in and out, like an enormous set of bagpipes. Wailing men, babies coughing, the sound of barking dogs. Melanie pressed her back into the farthest corner of the elevator, but she could not escape the noise.

And the worst thing of all was that the hallway was completely empty.

"My floor." The bellboy finally smiled, revealing a dark, toothless pit. Melanie could hear a vast roaring from deep inside him.

He exited the elevator and started walking down the empty, deafening hallway, the tray of food held high.

Melanie desperately pressed the "Close" button. She slapped at it over and over again until the doors finally started sliding together. Right before the two panels met Melanie thought she saw a chimpanzee with a human baby's face scuttle from one room to another.

Melanie stuck to the corner, as if it might somehow save her.

Fear froze her blood, her senses. Only her heart continued to pound inside her chest.

The silence of the elevator was unnerving. She could not discern the sounds of mechanical movement, and there was no telling which way she was really going. What if she was plunging through time and space? Who knew where the doors would open? What if she was going down and up, like an Escher print? Melanie started feeling sick. She glanced at the lights above the door, but she was still on the fourth floor.

The key card. She had to swipe it. Hand shaking, she dragged the plastic through the magnetic reader. "PH" lit up on the panel, and the car began to glide once more.

Melanie sagged.

It was exhausting. The terror was so very exhausting. The floor numbers lit up, one after the other, and Melanie watched with dread and impatience as she drew closer and closer to the penthouse floor.

Ting.

The doors slid open.

The cacophony of noise from the fourth floor had not followed Melanie to the penthouse level. She stared fearfully down the empty, brightly lit hallway.

The doors started to close and Melanie's hand instinctively shot out to stop the movement. Swallowing hard, head downward, she pushed the housekeeping cart and stepped into the long hallway.

Ornately patterned wallpaper writhed with unfurling fronds of fern and exotic birds in a pale hue. Melanie wondered if they were supposed to be gold. Mini chandeliers hung from the ceiling, and the crystals caught the light and scattered the fragments like strewn diamonds. Small, narrow wooden stands were laden with bowls of black, gray, and white flowers, and a few tastefully upholstered chairs were strategically placed in regular intervals. It was all so pretty. . . .

It was all so horrible.

Melanie's teeth started clacking. The noise was repulsive and she couldn't stop her mind's panicked associations. Bones clattering against bones. Skeletons jiggling up and down on puppet strings.

"Stop it!" Melanie hissed to herself. She began to push the cart down the dense, compact carpet. The wheels did not rattle.

She came to an abrupt stop.

The room card . . . she didn't know which room it opened.

Melanie stared down the hallway. There weren't that many doors: six in total. Three doors along both sides of the hallway were discreetly spaced in staggered intervals so no guest's door opened onto another's. She sighed with relief. Six doors weren't so many. And if there were guests in the room it didn't matter because she was Mavis, from housekeeping. She had a reason to be there. She took the swipe card out of her pocket and approached the first door.

Go on, she told herself. Go on. You can do it.

You can do it for your mum. For yourself. For everyone who

suffered in Half World. For all the tormented souls who were re-enacting their personal horrors for eternity.

Melanie was gripping the card so hard that it dug into her palm.

The pain sliced through her doubts and fears like a clean knife.

She took a deep breath and forced herself toward the unmarked door. She raised the card to swipe it in the magnetic reader, but then she paused. She thought for a few seconds and lifted her free hand and knocked on the door.

Silence.

Melanie slowly counted to ten.

Nothing.

She swiped the card.

One of two lights shone, but she couldn't discern the color. Agitated, she tried the door.

It did not open.

Melanie swiped again and tried turning the door latch more quickly, but it remained locked.

"Okay," she murmured. "It's okay. Just one down, five more left."

She got behind the cleaning cart and pushed it farther down the hallway to the second door. As she drew closer, Melanie raised the swipe card toward the magnetic reader.

When she heard an almost inaudible click.

Silence.

Melanie sucked in her breath and held, her heart double-beating inside her ears. She hadn't noticed, but there were tiny peepholes in the doors just above her line of vision. Her skin crawled. God, she thought, anyone could be staring out at her from behind the door. Anything . . .

Keeping her head down, Melanie tried to bring a close-lipped smile to her face. "Housekeeping," she mouthed hoarsely. She pointed to the vicinity of her name tag. "I'm Mavis," she enunciated, "your new housekeeper."

She thought she could hear a clicking. A familiar sound although she couldn't say where she'd heard it before. Something was spinning. A rotating device with hard metal pieces . . .

Like a roulette wheel in the casino . . . or the barrel of a revolver.

Melanie slowly, cautiously eased away, resisting the urge to raise both hands above her head. "I'll come back later," she whispered. "Sorry to bother you."

When she had crept away from the line of sight she heaved a great sigh. She could feel sweat turning cold upon her brow.

Suddenly, her hands started shaking. Her lips quivered spasmodically as delayed shock and adrenaline kicked in. She felt ready to collapse. Tears began to fill her eyes and she batted fiercely so she wouldn't ruin the makeup.

What was she doing here, a lone girl, without any weapons?

What did she think she could do?

Melanie dug the hard edge of the hotel swipe card deep into her palm, and the pain helped her pull back from the hopeless spiral.

"Don't," she hissed to herself. "It doesn't help. You can't change the past. But you can change the future."

Resolutely she pushed the cart toward the third door.

It burst open so suddenly she didn't have time to scream.

A bald portly man, bound hands held in front of him, a gag in his mouth and panicked terror and desperate hope in his eyes, was running toward her.

Something that Melanie couldn't see grabbed the back of him

and yanked him back into the room as if he were nothing more than a doll. Melanie could only witness the hope fade from his eyes before the door swung shut.

Every day.

This happened to the man every day. . . .

Melanie fought the urge to retch.

This was so wrong! How could this wrongness have continued for so long!

Somehow. She would try. She would try to make it stop.

Melanie approached the next door.

"Door four," she whispered as she drew closer. And despite the resolution in her spirit, her fragile mortal heart trembled inside her throat.

Door four. She so desperately wished she could pass by this door, marked with the unlucky number. . . .

How much can a person bear? she thought hollowly.

The silence of the entire penthouse floor was profound. Only the steady beating of her foolish heart.

As much as she had to, Melanie thought grimly.

She took a deep breath, swiped the card through the reader.

One of two small lights glowed and she heard the mechanism unlock with a loud click.

Melanie twisted the latch, and the door opened.

TWELVE

THE FOYER WAS dark but a diffuse light spilled around the corner of the hallway. Melanie stood in the half-light, gripping the handle of the cleaning cart in tight fists. A faint trace of something sour lingered in the air.

No more atrocities, she mouthed silently. Let this be okay.

The writhing threads of hope and terror were unbearable. She wanted to vomit.

Instead, she stepped through the doorway, pushing the cart in front of her as if it would somehow protect her. The door swung shut behind her.

The rubber tires squeaked overloud on the cold marble tiles. Melanie stopped.

"Hello?" she tried, her voice no more than a hoarse whisper.

She was inside. Suddenly her disguise felt horribly inadequate. As if she were a child who had been forced to design her own costume for the school play.

"Housekeeping," Melanie croaked feebly.

She was surrounded by silence.

Leaving the cart in the foyer, Melanie tiptoed down the hallway to cautiously peer into the living room.

The room was luxuriously decorated. The floor was covered in a rich, dense carpet, and the furniture was elegant and old-fashioned. Antiques, Melanie guessed, with finely carved arm-rests and curved legs, floral-patterned cushions. A low table, easy chairs, and a chaise divan were loosely arranged around a stand of bamboo growing in an enormous ceramic pot. A black grand piano was set near the heart-stopping wall-sized window. The lid was open but it barely seemed to take up any space in the sprawl-ing room. The massive framed oil paintings looked like postage stamps on the walls. Even in black and white the riches of the room were the grandest things Melanie had ever seen.

She released a long sigh of relief. No one was there, and she could quickly explore the room.

Glancing this way and that, Melanie stepped onto the carpet.

Two notes on the piano were pressed simultaneously in a quick three-beat succession.

Melanie gasped.

The same notes pressed three times again. Then two different notes, one, two, three, one, two, three . . .

The melody was bizarrely familiar.

Melanie stood at the edge of the living room, staring at the piano, the player hidden behind the raised lid.

"Chopsticks." The person was playing "Chopsticks."

The pianist played the notes that brought the tune back to the center of the keyboard to begin the piece once more. One, two, three, one, two, three . . .

Melanie did not know what to do.

And the piano player continued playing the maddening tune.

As if caught in a dream, she was pulled toward the hor-rible music. Her footsteps silent on the dense carpet, she drew closer and closer to the piano perched on the edge of the precipice window.

"Chopsticks" playing on and on and on . . .

Her heart filling her throat, Melanie moved around the piano to face the player.

The bench was empty.

She stared at the keys as they played themselves.

"Ha, ha, ha, ha," Melanie began to laugh weakly. "Hee, hee, hee, hee!"

"Who are you?" someone directly behind her asked.

Melanie shrieked and spun around, almost knocking over an open book on a book stand.

"Are you invited to the party?" the woman asked in a voice too slow.

Her hair was shorter, cut to her shoulders and curled under. Stark white foundation cast an eerie glow to her cheeks, and her lips had been drawn in with pencil and filled in more fully than their original shape. Dark mascara and heavy eyeliner lent a jaded toughness to her appearance, but her eyes were cloudy and unfocused. She seemed to be looking at a point just beyond Melanie's head.

Dressed in a black crepe dress that bristled with glinting shards of mirrors and jagged feathers, her plump arms were encased in long black transparent gloves that reached past her elbows.

In one hand she held an unlit cigarette. In the other was an empty martini glass.

It was her mother.

She had found her.

She had found her!

Tears filled Melanie's eyes. "Oh!" She could not speak; her heart was too full. "Oh! Oh!"

"Fumiko," a sticky voice cooed from the hallway.

A waft of pungent vinegar pooled into the room.

Melanie's heart froze. No! Not yet! It wasn't fair!

Her eyes darted behind her overlong bangs. She glared at her mother, willing her to know her. Can't you *feel* that it's me? she begged internally. Can't you see your own daughter, standing in front of you?

But her mother looked past her, and Melanie fearfully glanced over her shoulder.

Mr. Glueskin seemed taller than the last time she had seen him. And his face had changed yet again. Longer, leaner, he had raised the bridge of his nose and widened his brow. His hair was silver instead of white, slightly messy upon his high forehead. His white eyes gleamed. Dressed in a worn and ragged tuxedo, still ensconced in his stinking rubber boots, he looked like a groom who had deserted his wedding and had been on the streets for a very long time. In one hand he was holding heavily weighted plastic bags.

His middle was not bulging, as it would have been if he had swallowed up Gao Zhen Xi.

What had he done to her and Jade Rat?

Mr. Glueskin's expressive mouth curled with distaste as he caught sight of Melanie. "Well! About time help has arrived," he sneered. "We don't need housecleaning. But be the maid. What is your name, maid?"

Melanie, paralyzed with fear, could only stand there.

"Your NAME!" Mr. Glueskin roared.

"M-Mavis," Melanie whispered. "Mavis." She dropped her head, shoulders curling inward. Then her eyes fell upon her upside-down badge—

Horror dried all the moisture from her mouth.

Fumiko muttered something beneath her breath. Mr. Glueskin whipped his gaze away from Melanie to direct his attention at her mother.

"What, darling?" he asked in an overly kind voice. "What did you say?"

"Gladys," Fumiko monotoned.

Melanie's heart stopped.

Mr. Glueskin's eyes narrowed.

It's over, Melanie thought, her head dropping lower with despair. Like all the hopeless repeat women she had seen sitting on their cots in the dorm . . .

"Gladys," Melanie parroted. "Gladys. Gladys."

"Idiot!" Mr. Glueskin began giggling. He flicked her name badge with an overlong finger. "Your name is Glaaaaadys! You don't even know your own name! Ohhhh, good help is soooo hard to find. Maybe I should just eat you up and order up another maid instead?" He made a smacking, slurping sound and Melanie felt faint. She could scarcely stand.

Mr. Glueskin frowned. "No, it will ruin my appetite. For the lovely surprise party we're arranging for your daughter, Fumiko. Help the half-wit take the champagne into the kitchen." His tone suddenly changed. "They're getting warm!" he snarled.

Fumiko flinched, as if she had been slapped, then marched toward them like an automaton.

Mr. Glueskin thrust the bags at Melanie and she took them in her hands, lowering them quickly in case he could smell her Life beneath her layer of perfume.

"This way," Fumiko said, her voice flat.

Melanie trotted after her. Behind her long fringe of hair her eyes roved desperately for another exit. There had to be a secondary fire exit for such a large suite. She would talk to her mum in the kitchen and reveal her identity. And they would escape together.

They would go home.

Fumiko flicked on the light in the kitchen. The large island in the center of the room was covered with silver trays wrapped in cellophane. Little things writhed, squirmed desperately beneath the clear film. The gorge rose in Melanie's mouth.

"Don't unwrap these until all of the guests have arrived," Fumiko said emotionlessly. "Get ice from the freezer and chill the champagne." She pointed to the stack of dirty dishes in the sink. "Put those in the dishwasher. And polish the glasses by hand."

Melanie retrieved two bags of ice from the oversized freezer as she desperately tried to formulate a plan. She dumped the cubes into a large silver basin and placed four bottles of champagne to chill. Should she play at hired help and postpone saving her mother until another day? She could just continue with the guise, leave after her work was done, then come back to save her mother when Mr. Glueskin was away on his own frightful business.

Fumiko poured a large amount of gin into a martini shaker, her face completely vacant.

Melanie began placing dirty plates in the dishwasher to the sound of the alcohol being shaken with ice. Fumiko poured the stiff drink into her glass and took the straight gin down in one long swallow. She stared vacantly at the refrigerator for several seconds, then poured another big shot of gin into the silver shaker.

No! Melanie thought. If she waited any longer her mother might fall into an alcoholic living death just like her father.

Melanie spun toward her mother as she flipped her hair back to expose her eyes. She clamped down on her mother's gloved hand.

Fumiko glanced carelessly at the person who held her so fiercely. "What are you doing?" she asked tonelessly.

"Look at me," Melanie cried. "It's me, Mum. It's me!"

Fumiko's vague eyes slid over her daughter's intense gaze and gave a small shudder. She tried to pull her hand out of the maid's terrible grip.

"Why are you calling me that? I don't know you," Fumiko said in a monotone.

Melanie felt a rending in her heart.

"Mummy," Melanie wailed. "Don't say that!" Tears began to dribble messily down her face, and she crumpled gracelessly, circling her arms around her mother's legs. After all she had endured, after all she had done to find her. Melanie began to sob against the scratchy fabric of her mother's dress, the shards of mirror digging into her tear-stained face.

Fumiko inched backward, trying to shake the disturbed maid off her knees.

"No, Mummy." Melanie shuddered. "It's not fair." She raised her ruined face to gaze despairingly at her beloved mother. Melanie shook her head. "No! I crossed over into Half World to find you! I had to fight for my life! Watch people die. And I did it all for you!"

Her mother glanced at Melanie's disheveled frumpy hairdo,

the soggy, melted smears of black eyeliner and foundation.

Melanie self-consciously dragged the back of her hand under her mucus-smeared nose. The ugly and ill-fitting polyester uniform stretched too tightly over her chest and round belly.

Fumiko looked at a point somewhere over Melanie's shoulder. "You're deranged," her mother stated in a monotone. "You're mistaking me for someone else."

A tinny sound rang inside Melanie's ears. Somewhere, her heart seized, tight like a cramp, but the pain was someone else's.

A mistake.

Melanie staggered to her feet, grabbed Fumiko's shoulders, and pulled her close to her face. "See my eyes!" she hissed. "I'm alive! I'm asking you to come back with me to Life! You're *not* dead! You still have a chance! All you have to do is *remember.*"

Fumiko backed away from Melanie's hysteria, edging toward the door. "I couldn't possibly be your mother," Fumiko said flatly. "You're too old. You must be at least thirty."

Melanie's hands jerked upward to touch her own face. "It's just makeup," she babbled, trying to laugh. "It's just a disguise. Because I'm still *alive* alive. And you are, too! Not like everyone else in Half World." Her fingers brushed against something sharp and it bit painfully into the flesh of her cheek. She flinched.

Hands shaking, she stared at her fingers. Bright red against the black-and-white shades of Half World, marked with her living blood.

"What . . . " Fumiko whispered.

"Mmmm, mmmmm! I smell something tasty. I smell something fresh!" Mr. Glueskin called from the living room.

Melanie shuddered with revulsion. Oh, they had to get away.

And now she was marked. A small sliver of glass stuck from her finger. A shard of mirror from her mother's frightening dress. If she washed off the revealing blood she would expose the living tones of her skin. Was her face dotted with the brilliant red smears of a living thing?

Fumiko leaned closer, something changing in her expression. A brief moment—

Melanie grabbed both of her mother's hands. One of the fingers of her black glove flopped, empty. Her pinkie. It was gone.

Realization filled Melanie's chest with hot tears. "Mummy. You bit off your own finger. To get back into Half World. You did that to try to save me. . . . You have to come back with me," she whispered urgently. She pulled her toward the doorway. "Mr. Glueskin. He's tricked you. Remember, Mummy! I'm Melanie! I'm your daughter. Remember D-Dad? Shinobu Tamaki. You said you were waiting to see him again. That's why you never found someone else. You have pictures of Frida Kahlo and Escher! Bosch's paintings remind you of Half World." Her voice began to falter. "R-remember? You always said that I'm the best thing that's happened to you for all time. . . . You always said that. . . . " Her voice finally broke.

Her mother shuddered. She shook her head slowly, a great weariness sagging the flesh of her overpainted face.

"I do not know you," Fumiko said tonelessly. Her hands were dead things in Melanie's grip. "I have never seen you before in my life."

Melanie's nerveless fingers released their hold and her hands fell heavily to her sides. The weight of everything she had endured was more than she could bear. And she suddenly felt it all. The unspeakable despair was complete, and she finally understood how people could take their own lives, how her mother had suc-cumbed to hopeless sadness and become alcoholic.

The knowledge just didn't matter anymore.

"Leave," Fumiko said. "We'll find another maid."

A small sound slipped from Melanie's lips.

She had struggled so hard, suffered and endured. And for what? Not only was she rejected as a daughter, but she was un-wanted even as a maid.

She couldn't stand it.

Melanie began to laugh. She smacked her hand against her knee and laughed and laughed until tears ran down her face. She fell to the cool tiles, arms clamped around her sore middle, laugh-ing so hard that her shaking bordered on convulsions.

The high-pitched stink of vinegar poured into the room.

"Well," Mr. Glueskin said, "it's time to throw out this maid with the rubbish. She has gone mad."

Melanie opened her eyes to see Mr. Glueskin standing directly above her.

"What," Mr. Glueskin asked ever so slowly, "do we have here?"

The sharp prickle of her abraded cheeks began to burn.

Belatedly she pressed her hands to cover them up.

She could feel the stickiness of blood upon her palms.

Fumiko drew close to Mr. Glueskin and slipped her hand into his. Melanie felt sick as she watched his sticky fingers elongate and squeeze possessively, an elastic smile beginning to spread across his expressive face.

"Hello, Melanie," he said gently. "I'm so glad you could join us."

THIRTEEN

MR. GLUESKIN'S MOUTH seemed to move in slow motion, his elastic lips mouthing vowels with exaggerated care. It's funny, Melanie thought numbly. People look silly if you stare at their mouths and you don't know what they're saying. She stared vacantly as his words washed over her, morphing beyond meaning into malformed sounds. It was so nice not to understand....

"—fun games now!" Mr. Glueskin said, as Melanie returned to meaning with an elastic snap.

She blinked slowly.

Mr. Glueskin closed his hand into a fist and rapped the top of Melanie's head. "Hel-*lohhhh*," he inflected. "Anyone home? Dimwit! Nitwit! Half-wit!" He began clouting her skull, harder and harder with each word. Melanie could not stop the tears from falling from her eyes.

Why did her mother not stop him?

The doorbell rang throughout the suite.

"Oh! My first guests have arrived! We must welcome them. It's going to be sooo much fun!" Mr. Glueskin, one comforting arm around Fumiko, squelched his other hand around Melanie's wrist, melting his fingers and thumb into one seamless bond. Elongating his arm, he pulled her behind him like a dog on a leash. Melanie tried to pull out of his clasp but he yanked hard and she almost fell on her face.

Melanie followed.

Mr. Glueskin, Fumiko slightly behind him, stood at the door. He yanked downward on his arm-leash. "Sit!" he commanded.

Melanie, gritting her teeth, awkwardly lowered into a crouch.

Mr. Glueskin swung open the door.

A motley group of creatures stood at the entrance. A bird-headed man, naked except for a pair of faux fur shorts, a woman in a gown with eels instead of arms, a starfish with the face of a beautiful child at its tender center, wearing rubber boots, as if it was trying to look like Mr. Glueskin. The beauty queen pageant girl who had a hole in her face and her wallaby companion were there as well as several tall, twiggy bone people who clicked and clacked nervously in the background.

"My lovely friends," Mr. Glueskin said warmly.

"Hello!" everyone said simultaneously, as if they were an audience being cued in a game show.

Mr. Glueskin looked at each and every one, his expression growing tight, mean, as his gaze passed over them. "Where are my presents?" he asked in a completely neutral voice.

His friends looked down at their empty hands, at their neighbors' empty hands, and began to shuffle with agitation. Someone giggled nervously, "Hee, hee, hee—" until it was cut off.

Mr. Glueskin's pupils turned into tiny black pinpricks. "WHERE ARE MY FREAKING PRESENTS?" he screamed. His vinegar stink filled the air.

Melanie could scarcely bear watching. Fumiko, she noted, was looking down at her feet.

Horror filled Melanie's heart. What awful thing had Mr. Glueskin done to her mother? She had not thought about the time her mother had been forced to spend with this most despicable of creatures. She had been so dismayed that her mother didn't recognize her she hadn't given any thought to what her mother might have suffered. Melanie shook her head. Was it any wonder that she did not know her?

The cluster of "friends" at the entrance huddled together, like prey fish surrounded by predators. Just run! Melanie wanted to scream. Why didn't the fools just run? Why did they come here at all?

Because they are afraid, a tiny sober part of Melanie's mind assessed. This is what happens when you are ruled by fear. . . .

Melanie didn't know who or what it was, if it was an individual choice, or if some kind of silent decision had been made by the group, but suddenly the little wallaby with a man's head was thrust outside the protective huddle of the group. He stood there, exposed, his large dark eyes wide like a baby seal's.

"Awwwwww," Mr. Glueskin cooed. "You shouldn't have!" Something white flew, faster than the eye could track, and suddenly the wallaby's head was engulfed in an almost transparent skin of glue.

The party guests gasped simultaneously, then began to clap. "Hear! Hear!" someone called out with a jovial voice tinged heavily with relief.

The wallaby-man, unable to breathe, began hopping up and down, swiping with his front paws at the length of tongue that protruded from Mr. Glueskin's mouth. Choking, desperate for air, the wallaby-man tried to gasp, but the thin skin of the elastic tongue that covered his entire head bulged in and out of his own open mouth as though he were ineptly trying to blow bubbles out of gum.

Mr. Glueskin began to laugh. "Haw, haw, haw, haw!" He beat a rapid staccato with his stinking rubber boots. "Thaghhht kaw-cawwls!" he garbled.

He yanked back his tongue as he simultaneously unlocked his jaw, letting it sag, dropping open to his chest. For a moment the wallaby-man's bent back legs and tail stuck out from Mr. Glue-skin's mouth. His hind paws pattered their last, the tail swinging side to side.

It took several slow seconds for Mr. Glueskin to gulp him down.

Melanie, unable to help herself, dry-retched with abject horror. When she looked up once more Mr. Glueskin had a satisfied smirk upon his face, and his middle bulged as if he were carrying a baby.

"Come in! Welcome! We have a live show, today, and it's going to be spectacular!" He stepped aside so that the guests could file in. They caught sight of Melanie, the bright spots of blood upon her cheeks, and they stared with wonder as they began whispering among each other. The beauty pageant girl had somehow slipped away. She did not pass into the room. Maybe, Melanie thought grimly, she was going back to the kiddie zoo to wait for her friend to reappear once more.

The guests clustered together by the piano like a herd of nervous gazelle.

Mr. Glueskin stood back and stared at Melanie's housecleaning uniform with disdain. *"Che, che, che!"* he *ts*ked. "You look so ugly and you have so little to work with. You need to *freshen up*. You need an *outfit*." He began dragging Melanie toward a new passage. "You entertain each other for now," he called back to his guests. "Fumiko, get her a dress."

Mr. Glueskin tossed Melanie into the bathing room. It was enormous. Larger than the family living room of her home, it was completely covered in white tiles, silver chrome and black towels, the bathtub the size of a small swimming pool. A shower, large enough for a basketball team, took up the corner. Beside it was a lumpy white sack, like a laundry bag.

Mr. Glueskin spoke slowly and enunciated his words. "Bathe. Change your clothing. You're going to be the star of the show." He mimed showering and scrubbing, blinking dramatically, his tiny pinprick pupils so disturbing in the large polished whites of his eyes.

Melanie backed away. His moods were so mercurial. She did not know when he would fall into a fit of rage. When his joking would veer into violence.

Mr. Glueskin bowed low, several times, as he backed out of the bathroom. The door *snick*ed shut.

Rage flared inside Melanie's chest, threatening to burst up through her head. Her face flushed bright red with it. She wanted to beat him to a pulp. She wanted to punch his face in. She wanted to stomp his body until he was completely broken.

Melanie breathed hard and fast—

She covered her mouth with a trembling hand. How easy it was, after all, to turn into a monster.

Well, he would deserve it! a tight, mean voice inside her spat. The hateful and vicious things that he did, he would deserve everything that he got! Everyone would think so. He should die the way he lived.

Half lived . . .

Melanie wrapped her arms tightly around her middle. She caught sight of herself in the mirror.

Dark shadows encircled her eyes. Her eyes were bruises, wounds upon her face. She looked like she was close to thirty, not a teenaged girl. . . .

She looked an awful lot like her mother.

Melanie gave a ragged sigh.

Movement.

The white laundry lump writhed, stretched, like a larva wrapped in rubber.

The hairs stood up on Melanie's neck at the grotesque wriggling and humping. Suddenly, something poked outward, and the material stretched thin, transparent. Melanie could make out a foot, a leg, trying to kick out of the confines. A hand pawed against the white fabric—not fabric! It was someone encased inside a skin of glue.

She rushed to the trapped creature and tore at the material. It was drier than the skein of Mr. Glueskin's tongue that had bound her wrist. Melanie scratched and ripped at the white material and it seemed to grow stiffer, and finally she opened a seam. She grabbed the two edges and pulled her hands away from each other, the skin tearing like damp canvas.

Gao Zhen Xi's wrinkled face was soaked wet and pale like a cadaver's. Her hair was plastered upon her head, and the hand she extended shook with weakness. Melanie made to grab her wrist, but the worn old woman shook her head. She gestured with her chin and Melanie finally understood. She extended her own hand, palm upward, and Gao Zhen Xi sighed as she opened her closed fist.

The jade amulet felt sticky against Melanie's skin.

Gao Zhen Xi's mouth worked but words failed her. She gestured to her mouth, her throat, and Melanie dashed to the sink for a glass of water.

The old woman, still encased in the white skin, drank like it was the finest liquid in the world.

"Ahhhh," she sighed. "Thank you, child."

Melanie, eyes wide, nodded with relief. Gao Zhen Xi was all right. And she wouldn't have to face Mr. Glueskin and his horrible friends alone.

Gao Zhen Xi's eyes narrowed. "What has happened?"

Melanie's eyes filled, a wave of emotion washing over her at the sound of a concerned and strong adult voice. To feel relieved and inadequate made her feel so young and vulnerable. She wanted someone else, someone better than she was, to take over.

"I've found my mum. But she doesn't know me anymore. Mr. Glueskin has caught me—" Melanie's choked words were interrupted as the door banged open.

Fumiko, completely expressionless, threw a white gown at Melanie's feet. "Mr. Glueskin said to change into this," she said in a monotone. She returned to the raucous noise of the guests. Someone, not the program, was playing "Chopsticks" unevenly on the piano once more.

Melanie dragged the back of her hand across her eyes. "See," she whispered. "My mother doesn't know me anymore.

I shouldn't have come here. I shouldn't have bothered!"

"Melanie!" Gao Zhen Xi snapped. Melanie reared back.

"Your mother is caught in a trap. Half World should not be a trap for all who suffer, but because the Three Realms have been divided we cannot help but fall back, again and again, into a cycle of suffering. It is the same for your Realm and for the Realm of Spirit. We need the Three Realms reunited for there to be balance and wholeness. Without it we are all trapped creatures, only ever partially ourselves. No one is whole."

"What can we do?" Melanie asked, despairingly.

"What can you do?" Gao Zhen Xi asked softly.

"What do you mean?" Melanie crumpled beside the old woman on the floor. Her voice trembled. "Won't you help me?"

Gao Zhen Xi's head bobbed with weariness. "Child," she said gently, "you know not what our Half Lives have been in this Realm. Those of us who have some strength have somehow retained self-awareness; we can carve out a longer pocket of Half Life before we are flung back to our breaking moment. When we are thrown back the trauma and pain of that time is every bit as awful as when it first occurred in the Realm of Flesh. That is why so many here have become monsters. It takes much time to reach awareness that we are caught in that same loop once more. The realization is followed by despair. Many in Half World cannot rise above the despair. This is why your mother behaves as if she doesn't know you. She *doesn't* know you right now. She is caught in her trauma. She has not yet woken. And I—" Gao Zhen Xi's voice broke.

Melanie blinked anxiously. It wasn't just the old woman's voice that quavered. For a moment her substance seemed to shiver in and out of existence.

"I'm being pulled back once again." Gao Zhen Xi shook her head, her eyes more weary than ten thousand years. "Child, it is up to you. Only you are truly alive here. And with this Life you carry the capacity to change the pattern." The old woman seemed to grow transparent.

"Wait!" Melanie cried out, unable to help herself.

By some extreme act of will Gao Zhen Xi seemed to hold on to the fabric of her being.

"What must I do? I can't begin to know what to do! How can one girl change three Realms? I can't even stop Mr. Glueskin. I can't even save my mother." Melanie smacked her chest with the flat of her hand.

Gao Zhen Xi closed her eyes.

Melanie's rigid shoulders dropped. "I'm sorry," she whispered. She did not want to add to the old woman's suffering.

Gao Zhen Xi's eyes flew open. They glinted, momentarily, with a jade green fire. "It is not a matter of knowing the solution to righting all the wrongs. That is an impossible task. Even for one such as you." She smiled fiercely, and Melanie wondered at the respect in the old woman's voice. Respect, for her!

Despite the brief fire in her eyes, Gao Zhen Xi's voice began to grow faint. "It is only choice. In the end. When the moment comes. And it is a terrible thing. How will you choose?"

The elements that held the old woman together finally faded and she simply vanished, the sack of glueskin falling flat upon the cold white tiles.

Melanie slumped, alone.

FOURTEEN

CHOICES.

No magic words, no cure-all potion, no ultimate key that unlocked the prize door, no sorcerer's sword or special super latent power inside her waiting to burst free to save herself and her mother's life and everyone else in all three Realms.

Everything hinged on choices.

Her choices.

A flutter of panic tried to burst from Melanie's throat at the enormity, the overwhelming responsibility that bore down upon her. She took a deep, long breath and released it slowly. Twice. Three times.

She felt calmer.

She was not responsible for righting all the wrongs done to the Realms.

She was responsible for the things she chose.

That was all.

She almost managed a tiny smile. It was simultaneously an incredible responsibility and almost nothing at all, she thought wonderingly. "How remarkable," she whispered.

The jade amulet, still clutched tightly in her sticky palm, shuddered, and Melanie turned over her hand and unfurled her fingers.

The stone slowly shimmered from mineral to animal.

She was smaller than before. No longer the size of a small guinea pig, she was scarcely larger than a mouse.

"You're remarkable," Jade Rat said respectfully. She even bowed, and Melanie found herself bowing in return.

Then, solemnity fled as Melanie joyfully clutched her friend to her chest. "Thank you! You came back," she whispered. "You're so much smaller. Are you okay?"

Jade Rat snuffled Melanie's hand. "It is because much of the livingness of my Spirit was borrowed from Gao Zhen Xi's. Only a little remains within me. Soon I will revert to my stone self. But I will try to do what I can until then. I will try to seek help for you."

Melanie raised the small rat to her face and kissed her delicate nose. "Thank you. From all my heart."

"Don't give up your entire heart yet! I greatly doubt you have even fallen in love!" Jade Rat said sharply, sounding like her former bossy self.

Melanie blushed.

"I will turn back to stone. Flush me down the toilet. I'll escape out the septic system." The rat sounded confident, but her tail gave a betraying twitch.

"Brave rat," Melanie whispered. "Be careful."

With a tiny click, the rat turned into an amulet once more. Melanie did not hesitate. She flushed the jade pendant down the toilet. Her mouth dry, she watched the red strings swirl in the water before they disappeared.

"Choices," Melanie murmured.

Someone banged hard on the door. Melanie jumped around to face whoever entered, but the door remained shut.

"Ten minutes to showtime!" a muffled voice giggled.

Melanie stared down at her grubby self. She had nothing left to hide. She took a quick, hot, roaring shower. It felt amazingly good. She washed everything away, dried herself off, and put on the horrid white dress. It looked like something for a wedding, Melanie thought grimly, or for a sacrifice.

Her dark, wet hair hung straight to her shoulders. She parted her long bangs so that her face was revealed—so filled with Life, it shone like a beacon. Her cheeks were pink from the heat and her brown eyes glittered between amber and umber.

She would hide no more.

The party guests gasped when they caught sight of Melanie. In the black-and-white shades of Half World, she stood out like a golden candle in the darkest part of night. The sleeveless gown exposed her rounded arms, her ginger skin, and the flush of blood beneath the surface.

"Ohhhhhhh," the guests sighed longingly, as if they wanted to be like her, as if they wanted to have her. Their beady black eyes glinted, beaks clacked with desire and tails thumped the floor with a heavy and excited beat.

Mr. Glueskin, who had been playing with Fumiko the single most overplayed piano duet in school gyms everywhere, rose up from the bench with a loose and awful grin.

"Isn't she loveleeeeeeee," Mr. Glueskin sang. "Isn't she deeeelicious?" He released his tongue and it sailed fifteen feet across the room to land with a friendly *splat* upon her upper arm.

Melanie did not flinch.

He was licking her, she realized. He was trying to frighten her. That was his way. To toy with people, to trick them and terrorize them.

More than the actual suffering, what he wanted most was to witness the fear he inspired.

Melanie flicked the round blob of tongue that adhered to her skin. The tip sailed off and everyone gasped with shock as Mr. Glueskin sucked back his long tongue with a loud *snap*.

Fumiko, still seated on the piano bench, was staring out the wall of windows. White and gray neon lights flicked off and on in the Half World city, along with pale burning torches, gas lamps, and lanterns.

Melanie, after darting a glance, did not stare at her mother. Her mother was not being harmed, so it served no purpose to focus upon her.

Her purpose now was to reach Mr. Glueskin. To somehow reach his humanity. Because hadn't he been human, just like Gao Zhen Xi, even if it was so very long ago? He was not born evil. He had turned to evil. . . .

Melanie, unbowed, resolute, met Mr. Glueskin's inhuman eyes with her steady gaze.

The party guests held their breath. They stared, horrified, enraptured, at the dramatic tableau before them.

"Well," Mr. Glueskin said after several seconds had passed, "there is life in you after all. You wouldn't have thought it to see you so sniveling and pathetic earlier. Perhaps you will fight for your life fiercely, as we slowly drain it away. Your struggles, your pathetic efforts will entertain and delight us. Should we bleed you? Beat you? Drown you or eat you?"

Although her heart beat faster, Melanie did not look away.

"Should we feed you to your mother? Or would you like to take a little bite out of Mommy?"

Melanie flinched.

The party guests began whistling and applauding.

Mr. Glueskin bowed. "Thank you, thank you."

Melanie knew she could not withstand a game of cruelty against Mr. Glueskin. She had to take the ball. . . . She hated sports, stupid basketball with the layup tests, softball, volleyball, the cruelty of dodgeball.

Not a competition, she thought. Not a contest.

Time.

She should try to make more time for Jade Rat, who was looking for help. To rouse Gao Zhen Xi from her moment of trauma? Who else, in this Realm, had enough of their selves left intact to lend help to another? Someone, Melanie thought. If Gao Zhen Xi, after millennia, could still keep a part of her humanity, she had faith there would be others.

She would not try to beat Mr. Glueskin. She would befriend him. She would earn his trust by being compassionate. And he would come to see that there was nothing to be gained in breaking and destroying—that there were other ways of existing, even in Half Life. And after she had won his trust she would flee, forcing her mother to come with her if she had to.

Melanie bestowed a smile upon Mr. Glueskin.

The guests gasped in unison.

"Beautiful," someone sighed.

Melanie blushed at the compliment and the guests *ahhhhhhh*ed at her heightened color.

"Your home is beautiful." Melanie, sweeping her arm sideways, glanced at Mr. Glueskin from below her eyelashes. "And thank you for lending me this dress. I've never worn anything so lovely."

The guests swung their gaze toward Mr. Glueskin as though they were watching a tennis match. They looked uncertain of how they should respond, and they sought cues from his mobile face.

Mr. Glueskin's expression morphed from maliciousness to suspicion to jaw-dropped delight. "Darling girl," he mouthed with exaggerated care as he winked at his guests. "Fumiko, get your daughter a grown-up drink, why don'tcha! I think Half World agrees with her." As Fumiko silently went to the kitchen Mr. Glueskin turned to Melanie and crooked his long, thin finger to beckon her over. "I have something you might like to see," he whispered in a conspiratorial voice.

Melanie, keeping a smile on her face, casually approached him.

Mr. Glueskin looped his long, gluey arm through hers and led her toward an open book on a book stand. "I love literature, don't you?" He did not wait for Melanie's response. "Awfully uplifting. So satisfying and educational. Books make me feel so inadequate and inconsequential I just want to make a nice crackling fire with them to keep me warm at night!" He giggled with delight until something caught in his throat and he had to stop and bend over at the waist, to hack, snort, retch out a ball of phlegm. He spat a gluey mass the size of a golf ball across the room, and it splatted in the dead center of the starfish-child's face. She toppled backward, her many slow-moving arms trying to stretch her tube feet to remove the smothering mass.

The tall lady with the eel arms rushed to lend aid. The other guests just ignored them, so that they would not draw Mr. Glueskin's attention.

Rage burned hard and deep inside Melanie's chest, but she clamped it down. She could not overcome Mr. Glueskin and his guests with physical force. Time. She would bide her time. The starfish-child suffered, but she would not die.

The cruelty was that she would *never* die. . . .

"I love books," Melanie said lightly. "Especially antique books in used bookstores. They're like finding treasure."

Mr. Glue squealed with excitement. "You're going to love this!" Flecks of white spit flew from his lips as he skipped with excitement. "See! This is the oldest book I've ever seen," he whispered moistly in Melanie's ear. "It's filled with secrets and prophecies, and I want you to tell me what you see. Because they tell me the words change depending upon who reads them!"

A seed of dread swelled inside Melanie's throat.

The open book upon the stand: it was *The Book of the Realms*.

Mr. Glueskin began a singsong chant. "I found it! I found it! Nana nana booboo!" He yanked his friendly arm from the crook of Melanie's elbow and shoved her, hard, to the ground. Her knees skidded on the thick carpet, abrading the skin. Melanie did not cry out.

"Did you think you could sneak into this Realm without me finding out? Did you think you could save your mommy and go back home? You're an abomination! You should not exist! That you are here, in Half World, tainting the entire Realm with your Life, your capacity to affect changes, makes me CRAZY!" Mr. Glueskin shot upward, elastic, until his head nearly touched the ceiling, even while his jaw remained at its original height. Stretched out, hideously elongated, he was almost entirely mouth, arms, and legs. The stink of vinegar and mildew ballooned around him, stinging eyes and throats.

Snap! He contracted and then crouched down to draw Melanie up to her feet, a look of insincere concern etched upon his face. "Just think," he cooed. "All these years, a book of prophecy was right under my nose, inside this very hotel, and that hideous troll woman kept it from me! Intolerable! But now I know where she lives. I can visit her every day! It's all because of you, Melanie. I followed your stinking flesh. Did you know?" He cupped his hand around her ear, as if to speak to her privately, but his voice was raised for all to hear. "You have a really bad case of b.o."

Melanie's ears burned. Don't get triggered, Melanie told herself. He's trying to trick you into playing his game. Humiliation, she realized. It wasn't just terror and fear that he fed on—he also wanted to humiliate.

"I didn't know," Melanie said slowly. "Thank you for telling me. I'll be sure to pick up some deodorant as soon as I can."

The bony people and the bird-headed man looked nervously at one another, uncertain of Melanie's standing. The starfish-child, with the help of the eel-lady, had managed to pry off the clot of glue from her face. "Hurrah!" she cheered before the lady slapped an eel arm over her mouth.

Mr. Glueskin's pinprick eyes narrowed.

Melanie's heart gave a little flutter. The guests: all were not against her.

Fumiko returned with a bottle of champagne cooling in a bucket of ice and a tray of champagne flutes.

"Ah! Refreshments! Serve the bubbly, darling." Mr. Glueskin's tone was light and cheery.

The cork flew up with a pressurized *pop!* and the guests laughed too gaily.

Mr. Glueskin squelched his gluey hand at the base of Melanie's neck and forced her upward. Toward the book stand. He pressed her face to the open pages, much too close for her to be able to focus. The dark letters wiggled and swam like fish against a current.

"What do you see?" Mr. Glueskin hissed.

"I can't read it," Melanie said grimly.

He shoved her face into the page and rubbed her head from side to side. "Can you see it now!" he screamed. "Is that close enough for you!"

He released her so suddenly that she fell backward. The ceiling was so high above her, for a moment it swirled like a whirlpool. Melanie could hear the sound of champagne being poured into tall glasses, the individual bubbles popping, distinct, like microscopic musical notes. Mr. Glueskin's guests murmured, the bone people clattering like strands of wooden beads.

"Get up," Mr. Glueskin said kindly.

Melanie stood.

He pressed a slender glass into her hands and raised his own high. "Everyone! Everyone! I'd like to make an announcement!" The creatures grew silent and waited expectantly.

"C'mere, dollcake!" Mr. Glueskin stretched out an arm and tugged Fumiko into the crook of his vinegary armpit.

Melanie kept her face impassive. Only her hand holding the glass shook the tiniest bit.

"I'd like to welcome Melanie to my humble home and to Half World!" Mr. Glueskin began.

"Hear! Hear!" several people cheered.

"I'm not FREAKING FINISHED!" Mr. Glueskin roared.

The guests froze, silent.

"As I was saying"—Mr. Glueskin glared—"Melanie's arrival is so timely because Fumiko has agreed to marry me." He turned to his fiancée and gazed down upon her expressionless face with cloying adoration. "Haven't you, darling?" He gave Fumiko a little shake, and her head bobbled from side to side.

The guests politely applauded and cheered dutifully, but Melanie could scarcely hear a thing. A sheet of fire seemed to roar behind her eyes.

Her mother treated like this. Like an object. Like a *thing*.

Mr. Glueskin glanced at Melanie from the corner of his eye, his mobile lips smirking with glee.

Melanie inhaled deeply and slowly released.

Time. She would bide her time. She would not lose control. She had to convince him that she could be his friend....Jade Rat, she prayed. Come back to me.

Mr. Glueskin's eyes narrowed.

"Congratulations," Melanie said in an even voice.

Mr. Glueskin's thin nostrils flared. His pinprick pupils disappeared, and the whites of his eyes gleamed. "Drink!" he roared, and everyone quaffed their bubbly champagne. Melanie tipped the glass but kept her lips shut so that the liquid would not pass. She lowered her flute while everyone was still drinking and poured the contents onto the carpet.

"Melanie"—Mr. Glueskin leaned down to kiss her forehead; Melanie turned away and his sticky lips grazed her hair—"will be our little flower girl. After the ceremony, she'll be our roast suckling pig."

The bone people clattered nervously.

"Aren't you thrilled to be able to eat fresh suckling pig?" Mr. Glueskin seethed.

The cluster of guests broke into loud applause and whistles. "Roast pig! Roast pig! Roast pig!" they chanted, stamping their feet until the light fixtures clattered.

"Mmmmm, mmmmm good!" Mr. Glueskin smacked his lips, sliding his hand over his flat stomach. No longer bulging, the wallaby-man had been digested or yanked back to the kiddie zoo to begin his cycle once more. "I feel a mighty hunger! I have a mighty thirst! But first—" Mr. Glueskin latched his sticky hand to the back of Melanie's neck and propelled her toward *The Book of the Realms*—"I want you to read this out loud for our guests. This is the last bit of writing in the book. The pages that follow it are empty. So I want to know the last things it says. Share the future of your demise with us. Give us the gory details of what you see."

His tone. Mr. Glueskin sounded gloating and sadistic, but there was something else, too. He was uncertain....

Melanie's thoughts clicked inside her as her eyes skimmed over the words of the prophecy.

A child has grown
across the Realms

what divides draws
near. A child
may be reborn
so ends
what may
begin.

It had changed! Melanie blinked rapidly as she read it once more. The last time she had read it, it said something about an unborn child and then a child being born a second time. This version of the prophecy said the child had grown . . . she had grown! A glow of pride and sadness filled her heart. It was true, after all.

Her heart leapt. The prophecy also said what divides was drawing nearer. It must mean that they were closer to making things better. Surely it meant that! Her heart pattered like a little mouse.

The gluey clamp around the back of her neck stretched around to completely encircle her throat. The sticky elastic vise began to squeeze. "Read it, I said," Mr. Glueskin whispered.

"You first!" Melanie gasped while she could. "You tell me yours, and I'll tell you mine!"

Mr. Glueskin's eloquent face twisted from rage to fear to shame.

Melanie stared, amazed.

His eyes. They darted all over the page, corner to corner, side to side, but he was not tracking the letters.

Mr. Glueskin could not read.

FIFTEEN

HE COULD NOT read his own prophecy ... did not know what the future might hold. He couldn't be sure he was winning. ...

Where Melanie had hope, Mr. Glueskin was filled with doubt.

The rope of glue around Melanie's neck stopped her breath and white lights speckled and strobed in her vision. "Okay!" she choked. "I'll read it!"

Mr. Glueskin loosened his deathly grip, but did not release her.

Melanie, breathing hard and fast, thought rapidly. She cleared her throat then spoke aloud in a quavering voice.

> *All you have sought*
> *has been lost*
> *O child of woe*
> *weep, accept*
> *your fate lies*
> *in the hand*
> *of the new*
> *master*
> *obey!*

A sound burst out from between Mr. Glueskin's tacky lips. Guf-
fawing, he let his glass fall and dropped both hands to his knees as
he bellowed with maniacal joy. He smacked his wet palms against
his thighs and ran a stationary staccato with his feet. His vinegar
and rubber stink ballooned in the air. "Yes! Yes!" he crowed, hug-
ging himself with glee. "I knew it! I knew it! I knew those ru-
mors were false! No living things can be born into this Realm! I
stopped this grotesquerie from being born here, and now we will
kill her and eat her before the morning pale! Half Life forever!
For all eternity! We will erode the barriers between Flesh and
Spirit, and Half World will be the only cycle, for all time!"

Melanie could not stop the fear that rose in her gorge. Tonight.
He meant to kill her tonight.

Would she truly die? Would she be doomed to relive her suffering for all eternity? Melanie stared fiercely at Fumiko's profile.
Mother, she entreated inside her heart.

Fumiko slowly turned toward her.

Melanie could not decipher her expression.

Mr. Glueskin leapt to his feet. "More drink! Bring out the canapés! Music!" The doorbell pealed, and Mr. Glueskin clapped his
hands with excitement. He turned toward the foyer, but stopped.
Eyes narrowed, he whipped out a rope of tongue. The end snapped
around Melanie's wrists, binding them together, and he sailed the
middle of his tongue to loop around the leg of the piano. When
the post was encircled he broke off his tongue at the seal and
yanked the remaining portion back into his mouth.

Melanie pulled at her bonds.

There was an elastic give, but no way she could break free.

"Stay, piggy," Mr. Glueskin said as he went to welcome the new guests. Melanie heard the insidious inflections of his voice, the murmuring responses of both humans and inhumans. . . .

Melanie lowered the rope portion of her bonds to the floor. She stepped atop the tacky length with her feet and tried to pull both hands upward, but Mr. Glueskin's tongue did not snap, only stretched like rubber.

She sat upon the piano bench.

The room was beginning to fill up with Bosch-like creatures: fish-headed men, a puppy with a boy's face, hopping giant toads covered in bristling hairs, piglike simians and even some things that looked more plant than animal. Melanie didn't know if some of them had started out human and chosen animal parts or if they had begun as animals and chosen human parts. In the end, did it matter? The few humans who had chosen to remain so kept their death mark upon them: a gaping hole in the chest, pox-ridden pustules, gangrenous, stinking limbs. . . . Were they like Boy Scout badges? Melanie wondered. Did they compare them and brag?

Fumiko brought in more buckets of champagne on ice. The corks popped and guests squealed at the spray of bubbles. After topping empty glasses, she returned to the kitchen for the hors d'oeuvres. She brought the cellophane-covered silver platters into the room. Melanie could see things writhing against the plastic, little furred paws and tentacles and tails. When Fumiko removed the plastic, the little canapés leapt from the platter, scattering in all directions, and the guests shrieked with glee as they chased after their lively morsels. In the midst of the bedlam Melanie reached out to clasp her mother's arm as she passed by.

"It has to be tonight," Melanie said urgently. "It's going to be okay, Mum. We're going to get out of here. We can be okay. I believe." Melanie's voice caught in her throat. "And I love you."

Fumiko stood without any expression. When Melanie released her arm she walked away without a word. Melanie batted her eyes hard and fast. Maybe her mother heard her. Somewhere deep inside. She took a deep breath and released slowly.

And became aware that a crowd had gathered around her.

Sucking back the ends of twitching tails that dangled from their mouths, the Bosch people stared at Melanie like she was a freak of nature. They poked each other, giggling, sneering, sniffing the air around her with goat muzzles and feathery gills.

Someone stroked her bare arm. The touch was wet, slimy, like rotting ink-cap mushrooms. Melanie knocked it away with the flat of her hand, and the crowd of spectators gasped then tittered with nervous delight.

Someone yanked her hair. Claws prickled the back of her calf. Melanie jerked her leg away. The mob drew closer, eyes glittering, the stink of rotting flesh sweet and vile.

Melanie's heart pounded as adrenaline surged, a high ringing in her ears.

It had come so quickly. . . .

She bared her teeth. She would not die without fighting.

The starfish-child, her face like the center of a daisy, wriggled to the front of the pack. Her small eyes were round with concern, her lips downturned, wobbling.

"Mr. Glueskin!" she called out in a high, tremulous voice. "They're touching her and you didn't give them permission!" she tattled . . . and winked at Melanie.

Fear became understanding.

Her tormentor was the only one who had the capacity to protect her. Melanie bit her lip. It was too messed up. She stared into the eyes of the starfish-child. Thank you, she thought fiercely.

The starfish-child's rows of suction-cupped tube legs rippled with strong emotion.

Mr. Glueskin, cracking his tongue above their heads like a whip, broke through the mob. "Ingrates!" he seethed. "Pissant GREEDYGUTS!" he bellowed. The mob cringed backward like beaten dogs.

"S-sorry," a bone man stammered. "We're s-sorry, s-sir!" He bowed subserviently, and Mr. Glueskin kicked him aside. The bones fell to pieces, and Mr. Glueskin scattered them in different locations. A little dog-boy snatched one up and ran off.

"Hel-*lohhhhhh!* Ingrates! Freaks and idiots! Everything in its time, people! Everyone will get a piece of cake! Okay? Everyone will get pig cake! But not until I say so. And I get the FIRST PIECE!" he screamed, flecks of white glue splattering from his mouth. His eyes were alabaster orbs, a tiny prick of black in the center.

Mad, Melanie thought. He was completely mad. And everything he said—they were like the words of a twisted and tormented monster child.

What had made him this way? What happened when he was inevitably yanked back to the moment when he was horribly broken? Melanie shuddered with empathy and disgust. That he ended up so twisted, monstrous. . . . The evil done to him must have been unthinkable. The waves of revulsion and pity were overwhelming.

Mr. Glueskin caught sight of the emotions on Melanie's face.

Rage twisted his loose features. Contorting, seething, he dropped his jaw to the ground, his mouth flapping wider than his body, like a gulper eel.

Melanie stared down his maw. The moist acrid stink of vinegar burned her eyes, choking, vile and noxious. The skin inside his mouth, down his throat, gleamed white like larvae, threads of glue stringing downward like melting mozzarella. . . .

Mr. Glueskin unrolled his widened, flattened tongue, like it was a red carpet. When it was completely distended he wrapped the sticky tip lovingly and gently around Melanie's torso, pinning her arms to her sides.

He squeezed ever so softly, like the most kindly embrace.

Then began to gently pull her into his maw.

The rope of tongue he had bound her with melted back into the rest of his mouth. There was nothing to keep her from being swallowed into death.

A roaring filled Melanie's ears. She cast her eyes grimly for one last look at her mother's face.

There. Her profile. She was looking out the window. Distant and unreadable. The gown of mirror shards was actually very beautiful. . . .

Melanie would not go down without fighting all the way. She would wedge her legs sideways, she would claw with her nails, she would rip out the inside of his throat with her teeth.

The roaring grew louder, and the party guests looked about wildly, searching for the source.

The roaring was not inside Melanie's head—it was all around them, vast, thunderous, and awful.

The great wall-sized window crashed, shattered, splinters flying, screams and hooting laughter, the shards slicing into exposed skin, fur, scales, the roar swelling, a hurricane of sound, pouring, streaming into the room. Black, blackness, crows. Hundreds upon hundreds of crows, they buffeted the air, the whistling of beating wings, dark missiles swooping, swirling, pecking, scratching.

Melanie was tossed from Mr. Glueskin's tongue as an oddly shaped bird plunged to attack his eyes.

Melanie, on all fours, heart pounding, gazed upward.

Perched atop the large black diving crow was a tiny rat, her four long front teeth bared, clinging fiercely to pawfuls of feathers.

A joy-filled smile broke Melanie's face. "Yah!" she shouted hoarsely. She jumped and shook both fists in the air. "Yahhhh!"

Five birds had landed atop Mr. Glueskin's head and were pecking at his eyes, tearing at his ears, and stabbing his cheeks.

Swarms mobbed the party guests, some of them fleeing with arms windmilling around their skulls, others trying to duck low and crawling upon the carpet. The bird-headed man in the faux fur shorts clacked his sharp beak, *snick*ing a leg off a crow. It screamed before spiraling to the ground. The bird-headed man trampled it beneath his coarse bare feet.

Crows plucked individual bones off the bone people until they finally crumpled like stacks of wooden sticks. The starfish-child had pulled her many arms inward to cover her tender face, her bumpy, hard exterior a protective armor.

Fumiko crouched beneath the piano. Face blank, she plucked shards of glass from her pale cheeks, dark spots of blood dotting her skin, spreading.

Snap! Snap! Snap! The air cracked, and crows dropped, fell, as if they had been shot.

Mr. Glueskin wielded his tongue like a whip, flicking the tapered tip faster than the eye could follow, even as he netted the birds around his head with a fine skin of glue shed from his palms.

Crack! The largest crow fell like a stone, and Jade Rat leapt from its perch upon its shoulders and landed on the carpet. The rat dodged as a man toppled sideways, the swarm of crows attacking his death badge, a wound in his stomach. They pulled and yanked at his entrails.

Melanie could see a clear path between her and the piano. She pelted through. Something stabbed, hot and red, into the bottom of her foot.

Glass. The fragments from the shattered window. It lay in an outward-spreading arc from the open frame, a cold wind beginning to keen, and far, far below the honking of distant cars, the spiral wail of sirens, the braying of donkeys and snarling dogs, screaming.

Teeth gritted, Melanie pulled out the long sliver of glass that was embedded in her heel. Luckily it had not gone through a softer area of her foot. It would have pierced her like a nail. Her rich red blood shone bright, almost glowing, in the black-and-white world. Melanie stared at the half circle of broken glass that surrounded her mother, stared down at her now-bare feet. Her mother wore shoes; she could walk through. Melanie stretched out her hand slowly, palm upward, as she would to a small, troubled child. "Come with me," she said gently. "It's time to go."

Fumiko looked at her with wide, blank eyes. The dark spots

of blood on her cheeks looked like smeared ink. She slowly gazed upon the melee in the room. The whirring rush of hundreds of wings, the yelps and screeching of people fleeing from the birds, feathers drifting down like black ashes. Fumiko slowly reached out for her daughter's hand.

Mr. Glueskin roared. "Mine!" he screamed. Cracking, snapping, the sounds were percussive as he took out crows three, four at a time, forcing his way toward them. "Mine! Mine! MINE!"

"We have to go," Melanie said more firmly, keeping the desperation out of her voice. She held her mother's gaze and even managed a smile. "It will be okay."

Something hopeful seemed to slowly bloom in her mother's eyes. For the first time since she had seen her in Half World, something of the mother she knew was returning.

White glue splatted upon Fumiko's face, engulfing her features, her head snapping back with the impact.

Melanie screamed.

Fumiko instinctively clawed at the thick skin of glue that covered her nose and mouth.

Mr. Glueskin whipped back his tongue like a chameleon, and Fumiko was yanked from the shelter of the piano to be dropped at his feet.

He slowly began lowering his jaw, sagging, yawning wider and wider, his head disappearing, until all that was left was a gaping open maw.

Noise faded to a distant roar while ever so slowly, birds flapped, as people toppled beneath dark swarms. As if a broken projector were playing an old-fashioned film, the world around Melanie seemed to stutter like a series of stills, movements strobing, the seconds between realities frozen.

Melanie located calm.

Her eyes swept over her surroundings. Broken glass from the window.

Glass would not sever the elastic bonds that smothered her mother. The bottle. No. Mr. Glueskin would just re-form. He had no skull to shatter.

Waving her eel arms about her head, a woman ducked with excruciating slowness, falling toward Melanie.

Melanie slow-motioned sideways, to avoid being knocked over, and her foot stuck to something sticky in the carpet. She lifted her foot and the blob of glue stretched like freshly chewed gum.

Like gum . . .

The world accelerated, with the thudding rush of wings, screeching party guests, Fumiko inexorably dragged into Mr. Glueskin's cavernous mouth.

Melanie spun around. She grabbed the neck of the champagne bottle and tossed it to the side. She snatched the bucket of ice and melted water. She leapt over the quivering bodies of fallen birds, sidestepped people being pecked to pieces. She planted her feet in the threads of the carpet and dashed the contents of the bucket onto Mr. Glueskin's tongue.

SIXTEEN

WITH A BEAUTIFUL crinkling crystalline sound, half of Mr. Glueskin's distended tongue grew stiff and solid. Though it was still attached to the back of his soft mouth, he could no longer control its motion. The weight of Fumiko, still attached to the gluey chameleon tip, pulled his numbed tongue to the floor. Fumiko, flopped onto her side, desperately tore at the skin of glue that still covered her face.

Mr. Glueskin's features seeped back into place, his white eyes rolling wildly, rage and frustration stretching his face monstrous. Unable to control his frozen tongue, he began creeping his mouth forward, toward and around his frozen flesh, like a constrictor rippling its body around its prey. He inched his maw toward Fumiko, whose struggles were growing weaker.

Jade Rat spat out the ligaments of someone's detached eye. It tumbled on the carpet until it came to rest against a dead crow. "Yes!" Jade Rat cried jubilantly. "Ice!"

Melanie snatched up a second bucket, a third, and threw the contents onto the tip of Mr. Glueskin's tongue and further down his throat with a great rattling splash. As the cold spread, he slowly lost all elasticity, the flexible bonds growing stiff, hard, until his face was frozen into an enraged mask.

Fumiko twisted and Mr. Glueskin's tongue broke off with a snap, a third of the way down, like a dry branch breaking off a tree.

The stump of frozen tongue fell into pieces. They looked like irregular chunks of firm white cheese upon the carpet of black feathers.

Belatedly, Melanie's heart began to pound triple time. She gently pulled the hardened glue from her mother's face and it came off like plaster of paris. She tossed the mask aside.

Melanie stroked the sweaty strands of hair away from her mother's face.

Silent.

Then, her mother began to cough and cough.

Everyone was still. Birds, party guests, beasts, and monsters. They stared at the tableau, shocked into paralysis.

Mr. Glueskin had been disabled.

By a girl with buckets of ice.

Melanie helped her mother into a sitting position and gently rubbed her back. When she could breathe evenly, she helped her mother rise to her feet. Her hands were trembling.

Melanie said nothing. She threw her arms around her mother and held her, hard. She could feel her mother's heart pounding against her.

Fumiko slowly lowered her head to rest upon her daughter's shoulder.

Jade Rat shrieked.

Melanie jerked. Caught sight of her small friend.

A clot of tongue, slowly melting, was trying to stretch back toward Mr. Glueskin's mouth. It looked like a white leech, inching its way to its master. The rat had clamped her teeth into the lump even as it strained to worm away, the rodent digging her four paws into the threads of the carpet.

All of the scattered pieces of tongue were melting, and they were trying to inch their way back toward the stump that still remained frozen within Mr. Glueskin's mouth.

Mr. Glueskin wriggled his loosening eyebrows. He waggled them like he was an old-fashioned comedian. "Ghhhhheeeeeeeee-uuuuuuuuuuuuu!" he groaned, his voice deeper than a fog-horn.

Not enough! Melanie's heart stuttered. It wasn't enough.

No one stopped her as she dashed to the kitchen.

She flung open the freezer and found large plastic bags of ice. She grabbed all three of them as well as an empty ice bucket as she ran back to the thawing Mr. Glueskin. Melanie ripped open one bag and clasped several handfuls, dropping them into the empty bucket.

The lumps of melted tongue slimed toward Mr. Glueskin's open mouth like homing slugs. Melanie snatched them all off the ground and plunged them into the bucket of ice. Instantly hardened by the temperature, they became inert.

Mr. Glueskin was thawing, his neck gaining mobility, and he turned toward her. His stump of tongue began to protrude, like a slow gray slug. He began to smile.

Melanie dug her thumbnail into another plastic bag and tore it open. Loose cubes tumbled to the carpet. She grabbed a handful from the open bag and shoved the rough ice into Mr. Glueskin's open mouth.

The bottom half of his face locked with the cold.

Mr. Glueskin's eyes seethed with hate, but Melanie stuffed the remainders of the bag into his hardened maw.

"Good thinking," Jade Rat sighed with relief. "Now get a knife."

Melanie jerked with shock. Then resumed pouring the ice in a circle around Mr. Glueskin's feet. Her face twisting with distaste, she pulled his collar away from his neck to drop ice cubes down the front of his shirt until he was completely surrounded and filled with ice. "No," Melanie said slowly. "We can't kill him."

Mr. Glueskin was solid. Even his eyes had ceased moving. He looked like a poorly made sculpture for a parking lot carnival.

"Why not?" Jade Rat panted. Her sides heaved with exhaustion and she was scarcely bigger than a shrew. "He would have done the same to you, even worse. If we let him live he's going to come after you again. We have to end it now."

Melanie poured ice into his large rubber boots, then, wrinkling her face with great disgust, let the frozen cubes rattle down his waistband. The plastic bags were empty. Mr. Glueskin was completely frozen.

Until all the cubes melted.

How long would it take?

Melanie looked up.

Everyone was looking at her. The party guests who had remained to fight the crows. The birds that were still alive. The starfish-child's face was exposed, her mouth hanging open with wonder and awe. The woman with the eel arms stared at her from the carpet, the black sinuous skin of her limbs writhing with confusion. The bird-headed man's beak *snick*ed with agitation.

In the stillness, Melanie could hear the *click, clack* of dry bones trying to pull themselves together again.

Her mother. Coming toward them from the kitchen. The shards of her mirror dress glinted like a stream, some of the larger pieces reflecting, for microseconds, the carnage around them: dead twisted crows, empty eye sockets, mounds of feathers, and pools of black blood.

Fumiko moved like a sleepwalker, a meat cleaver held high above her head. Her dark eyes were blank, dead, the splotches of blood upon her cheeks black and inky.

Melanie's heart clenched hard into stone.

What had her mother become?

Fumiko stopped beside Mr. Glueskin. Expressionless, wordless, she let the weight of the meat cleaver fall toward the back of his exposed and frozen neck.

"No!" Melanie, ducking between them, caught Fumiko's wrists with her hands.

Fumiko did not respond. She did not fight her daughter, but she seemed to be caught in a sleepwalker's motion. She continued to press down, as if the steely blade were being pulled toward Mr. Glueskin's vulnerable neck.

"No, Mother!" Melanie cried out. "We must not do this thing!"

"How will we stop him, then?" Jade Rat said hoarsely. Melanie could scarcely hear her voice. The rat sounded so weak, but Melanie dared not look at her. She could feel her arms beginning to quiver as her mother bore downward.

"He will melt. Then he will begin again," Jade Rat whispered. "We must cut him into pieces and scatter them throughout this Realm. Bury the pieces deep. Anything."

Something clicked inside Melanie's mind. "That's just it!" Melanie cried. "It doesn't matter if we destroy him. The cycle will repeat, even though we've done this horrific thing. He will start back at the beginning of his cycle, no matter how far we've scattered his body. It's not his body that has to be broken. It's the cycle!"

A silence rang.

Like a deep bell, like circular ripples expanding in a pool of water. In the distance they heard a mournful mewing. The sound was muffled, and they strained their ears to pinpoint the source of the sound.

A cat, perhaps, in the neighboring suite?

The mewling was slowly growing louder.

A *crinkle, crinkle* of sound, of something brittle beginning to break.

The floor lurched, the ceiling swaying, and Melanie staggered with sudden vertigo. People, creatures cried out with fear, threw themselves to the floor on all fours for greater stability.

Fumiko's grip slipped and the heavy cleaver fell, fell, ever so slowly as Melanie stared with horrified eyes, the great silver blade spinning a slow three hundred and sixty degrees to embed, blade first, sinking a few inches into Mr. Glueskin's head.

Mr. Glueskin's body tottered, and it was enough. He began to tip backward like a falling statue. He landed on the carpet with a soft thud, lolling a little from side to side, as solid as stone, until he came to a rest.

They stared at his frozen form, the cleaver stuck in his head.

It was so horrible. It looked almost comic.

Melanie was simultaneously swamped by nausea and hilarity.

A loud *crack* split the air, as loud as cleaving alabaster, and they all gasped, leaping backward.

As if something under great pressure had finally been breached, Mr. Glueskin split from his head downward, his clothes parting, to expose a white, bloodless vertical seam in his abdomen.

The mewling cries grew louder, rasping with urgency.

They leaned in close to see. . . .

A wet *crack!* Mr. Glueskin, hard as a peach pit, split wide open to reveal a tender center.

A great wind roared about Melanie's head, whipping her hair, and she staggered against her mother's body. Just as suddenly the air stilled. The perpetual reek of vinegar had disappeared. A baby cried, loud and healthy.

They stared, shocked, speechless, at Mr. Glueskin. His hardened white body had cracked in two. He had no entrails or bones; he was solid white all the way through. And in splitting he had exposed a small baby. Pale, faintly pink and luminescent, the infant seemed furiously alive, kicking the air with his tiny heels, tiny hands squeezed into tight fists. A moist, sweet fragrance of rising bread. . . .

SEVENTEEN

JADE RAT STOOD upright on her haunches, her tiny paws crossed upon her chest. Her voice was small, but she spoke clearly with reverence and profound completion.

> *A child is formed and leaves*
> *unborn*
> *a flight across the divide*
> *When she returns*
> *so ends what should*
> *not be*
> *a child is born*
> *impossibly*
> *in the nether Realm of Half World.*

The tiny rat wavered for a microsecond, then with a barely audible click, she fell back to the carpet, an amulet once more.

The infant's cries were growing stronger. Mr. Glueskin's guests shuffled nervously backward, muttering among themselves.

Melanie glanced anxiously at their human and inhuman faces.

Was the prophecy complete? Had the Realms been reunited?

Were she and her mother free to return home?

The baby continued squalling, and Fumiko shook her head. The noise seemed to rouse her and she frowned, as if waking from the depths of someone else's dream. She raised her head and caught sight of her daughter.

"Melanie?" she asked, her voice tinted with alarm, surprise. "Melanie?"

Melanie's face lit up, like a flower facing the sun.

Fumiko raised a trembling hand to cup her daughter's jaw.

Melanie closed her eyes and hot tears trickled down to pool inside her mother's palm.

"This is wrong," a creature hissed.

"Mr. Glueskin will blame us when he comes back!" a second voice grunted.

"We must do something," someone hoarsely urged.

The bird-headed man clacked his predatory beak. "In his cycle, he was killed by his father while his mother was trying to birth him. That's the cycle that formed him. That's the cycle that he stretched. He was the first who understood that we could change, stretch, reshape our Half Lives."

The eel-armed woman nodded her lovely head. Her dark eyes gleamed with feeling. "He was trapped, as a baby, almost born, but always dying. But over hundreds and hundreds of years, he built upon his knowledge. Until the victim became the killer!"

The bird-headed man's feathers stood upright with great agitation. "He is our savior! He showed us how we could become powerful, even though we are thrown back to our original trauma once more!"

The eel-lady wrapped her slimy limbs around her lithe torso. "I would still be in the sea, drowning, if it wasn't for Mr. Glueskin," she whispered.

The bird-headed man tilted his head to one side, his gray eye glinting, unreadable. "He must not be allowed to be born again. Not like this! It goes against everything that he has become! If one cycle is broken who can say what will happen to ours?" He took a step closer to them and Melanie heard a small *crunch.*

"No!" Melanie cried out. She shoved the bird-man, hard, and he staggered several steps backward. Melanie crouched down, her heart thumping loudly.

A piece still remained attached to the length of red string. But half of the jade amulet had been crushed into fragments.

Jade Rat—broken.

Melanie's lower lip wobbled. I'm sorry, Gao Zhen Xi, she thought. I'm sorry, Ms. Wei. I'm so sorry, Jade Rat.

Melanie snatched up the string and wound it around her wrist, leaving the ends to be clasped inside her hand. She began backing toward the snuffling baby. She could feel her mother doing the same.

Melanie held out her free hand, palm outward. "Wait," she implored. "Can't you see? We *need* to change the cycle. You have all been trapped in suffering. But it doesn't have to be this way!" With her peripheral vision she could see crows quietly hopping toward her.

"You *child*," the eel-armed woman snickered. "This is our Half World. This is all that we know." She bent down low, her eel arms writhing wildly. She dropped open her mouth to reveal a stubby black eel tongue. It had eyes and a mouth lined with fine needle teeth. "This is all that we want!" the eel tongue squealed.

Fumiko snatched Baby G from his shell and yanked the back of Melanie's dress. "Run!" she shouted just as all of the crows upon the carpet burst upward, creating a thunderous black wall of wings.

The party guests reared back from the burst of motion, and Melanie, the amulet clutched tightly in her palm, ran with her mother through the front door and into the corridor.

Stairwell, Melanie thought frantically. To the roof of the building. Back to the mountain and the bridge of crows.

The crows. Belated tears of gratitude filled her eyes.

She spun toward the sign that marked the fire escape.

Fumiko pulled her toward the elevator. "This way! I remember!" she choked.

They could hear the din of voices, snarling, bleating, the rush of wings.

Melanie, after a moment's hesitation, ran with her mother toward the paired doors.

"Down!" Fumiko cried.

Melanie pounded the button. "Come on!" she begged. "Come on, come on!"

From behind them the pitch of voices changed, growing jubilant and frenetic. For the first time, the crows began to caw. They cawed and cawed, the sounds of their cries growing distant, then disappearing.

Melanie and her mother heard Mr. Glueskin's door opening just as the bell tinged the arrival of the elevator.

They rushed into the car, and as Melanie pounded on the "Close" button they stared down the hallway.

The door to Mr. Glueskin's suite was open, but something was blocking the exit.

A strangely formed thing, holding back the mob with numerous triangle-shaped limbs.

It was the starfish-child; her bumpy armor top turned to the rage of the mob, Melanie could just make out her daisy face profile. She was smiling bravely. "Hurry!" she urged as the elevator doors began to shut. Just as one arm, then another, was ripped from the starfish-child's body.

Melanie sobbed.

Fumiko, eyes grim, Baby G clasped to the left side of her chest, pressed a button on the panel.

The number four lit up.

"No!" Melanie cried. "What are you doing! The fourth floor is evil!" She tried to push the "Emergency Stop" button, any button, but her mother seized her arm in a fierce grip.

"Stop it!" Fumiko said sharply.

Melanie recoiled. She had never heard her mother sound so forceful before.

Baby G began whimpering and Fumiko jostled him comfortingly. "I'm sorry, Melanie," Fumiko said softly. "But it's the only way back to your Realm."

Melanie sagged back against the cool wall. Of course. It made sense, really. She looked up at the ceiling, wondering how quickly the second car would reach the mob. "What are you going to do with the baby?" she asked. Her feelings writhed, complicated, confused.

Fumiko shook her head. "I don't know. But he cannot be left here to fall back into his cycle."

The elevator seemed to cushion itself, and the bell tinged before the car came to a complete stop.

They were stopped on the thirteenth floor.

Fumiko looked at Melanie sharply.

"I didn't touch it!" Melanie exclaimed.

Futilely they pressed themselves against the back panel of the car.

The doors silently slid open.

A pale suit, outdated and too small, did little to hide an untucked dirty T-shirt, a beer belly flopping over the cinch of belt. A crumpled five-dollar bill had been crammed into the buttonhole. Clinging to the man's arm was a beautiful woman with long black hair, wearing a floor-length black gown. Her eyes were completely rolled back in her head. Only the whites showed, gleaming wetly.

The man leaned a little too far forward as he winked one of his small watermelon seed eyes. "We got off on the wrong floor," he enunciated carefully. "We've been invited to a party in the penthouse!"

"Shinobu!" Fumiko cried, her voice as wild as a falcon.

The man reared back. His pale face blanched completely white. He blinked and blinked, shaking off his companion's hand to rub both of his eyes with the heels of his palms.

Fumiko thrust Baby G into Melanie's arms.

Instinctively she cradled him.

"I'm sorry," Fumiko said grimly, and pushed Shinobu's date, hard. The woman fell backward onto her bottom.

Fumiko grabbed Shinobu's crusty lapels and yanked him into

the elevator. She pounded the "Close" button and the car began descending once more.

Melanie stared at her mother and father. She had never seen them together. They both seemed like strangers.

Shinobu stood gaping at Fumiko. A light beginning to grow in his eyes. He blinked and blinked with confusion. Wonder.

Lips quivering, Fumiko smiled, beautiful.

Tears filled Melanie's eyes as she watched years falling from her mother's face as her mother continued gazing upon her father.

"Remember?" Fumiko asked him gently. She turned toward her daughter and stretched her hand to stroke Melanie's cheek with infinite gentleness. "Our daughter, Shinobu. Our daughter, Melanie."

"She's alive," Shinobu's voice trembled. He slapped his own face, hard. The sharp sound startled them all. "Is this happening? I've been lost for so long." His voice began to crumble. "Fumiko . . . "

Fumiko enfolded Shinobu with her arms. "It's been fourteen years," she murmured into his dirty hair. "Our daughter grew up in Life, even though we do not hold Life ourselves." She shook Shinobu and he raised his head.

Pride shone from his eyes.

"We have done well," Fumiko murmured, "but it is not over yet."

The elevator sagged then cushioned a few inches upward before it came to a stop.

Ting.

They were on the fourth floor.

"Not again," Shinobu's voice was low. Weary.

"No," Fumiko whispered. "It's different this time."

The doors began to slide.

Too late, Melanie remembered the barrage of awful noise. Her shoulders tensed instinctively, and the baby in her arms, sensing her change, stilled.

The doors opened to utter darkness. Silence.

Baby G gave a soft sigh.

Shinobu swallowed loud enough for everyone to hear. He cleared his throat. "Whose baby is this?" he asked hoarsely.

"Not mine!" Melanie said sharply, her ears burning. "It's Mr. Glueskin! He was born again!" As her words sank in, Melanie couldn't stop a small giggle from escaping.

The darkness engulfed the sound.

"Shhhh," Fumiko cautioned.

The light from the elevator should have been cast outward, to reveal at the very least the floor of the hallway, but it was as if all light were swallowed. They could not discern any shape or shadow. They could not know if anything even existed beyond the open doorway.

Melanie's heart tripped. What was out there? There was no way to tell if a hallway existed at all. Maybe it was an enormous room and things, creatures, monsters were all staring at them, exposed like actors on a tiny, brightly lit stage. Maybe they couldn't attack until they entered the dark. They would be torn to pieces, limbs strewn, and devoured.

A mechanical grinding.

They twitched, hypersensitive, and stared fearfully at the darkness. As realization set in, all three simultaneously stared up at

the ceiling of the car. The clinking and whirring were the sounds of an elevator car descending....

The mob must have waited to see which floor they stopped at. And now they were coming.

Melanie squeezed her hand around the broken edge of the jade amulet. She glanced down at the pink baby in her arms. His eyes were closed and he had both middle and ring finger stuffed inside his mouth.

Melanie took a deep breath and stepped out of the elevator. Fumiko grabbed a small handful of cloth at the back of her dress, and Shinobu clasped Fumiko's hand so that wherever the darkness took them they would be together.

EIGHTEEN

THEY SHUFFLED IN the utter blackness. Even Melanie's Life had no powers to bring light into the unspace. That there was something upon which to place their feet, upon which to walk, seemed miraculous, and each foot raised was a surge of despair, each step placed a gasp of relief.

Melanie looked back, once, just as the elevator doors closed, the rectangle of light growing thinner until it disappeared. When she looked forward, she was no longer certain if it actually was the same direction they had been moving. In the absolute darkness there was no up or down or markers of time. The only intervals were their heartbeats. . . .

Melanie's footsteps faltered, came to a stop.

Baby G was warm in Melanie's arms. His living heat was an anchor. The rough, broken edge of the jade amulet felt real inside her fist. And the tug of her mother's hand at the back of her dress grounded her, if only a little bit.

"I-I don't know which way to go." Melanie's voice sounded simultaneously insignificant and overloud in the absolute silence.

Fumiko flattened her palm upon Melanie's back. "I'm frightened, too. But I think this is the right way because it's not the same as before. Everything has changed."

"You can do it," Shinobu called from behind. "If you've come this far, if you've managed to change Mr. Glueskin's cycle, it can't be the wrong way."

Melanie swallowed. They could not stand there, in limbo, forever. Or maybe they could. But she did not want it. After all they had gone through! To remain there, immobile, broken out of the cycle, only to be stopped by fear?

No.

Melanie took a step in the direction she thought was forward. Her mother, clasping a small handful of material at the back of her daughter's dress, came after. Melanie took another step. The ground remained firm. She took a third step. The fourth—

A vast roar filled the air. Their hair buffeted upward with the surge of wild wind. Melanie could not breathe. She desperately clung to the baby, who was almost ripped from her arms with the immense force.

The blackness that had completely surrounded them suddenly sheered away. The absolute darkness split apart into black strands against a slate gray sky. Crows, so many ribbons and ribbons of swooping, cawing crows, jubilant and raucous, veering away toward a far pale horizon.

Melanie could feel the slightly oily softness of feathers beneath her bare feet. The buoyant give of the bridge, beginning to wobble and undulate. At once familiar and awful. She began to run.

Panting, gasping, she pelted across the glossy backs of the crows, so dense she could not see the emptiness of space below her feet. But the bridge was narrow, scarcely five feet across. In the growing light she could see the lone mountainside, the rocky ledge in front of the Gate. She could no longer feel her mother's hand clasping the back of her dress.

Were they still there?

The backs of the crows felt as slippery as stones in a river. The rush of cold air numbed her feet, her toes, and she felt weak, the weight of the baby bearing her down. The air roared with the beating of countless wings, like a flash flood careening down a steep canyon.

Her arms held Baby G more firmly as she kept on running, the living, flying bridge weaving, undulating. The drowning roar.

Almost, she promised herself. Almost there!

"Oh!" she heard her mother gasp.

Relief that she was still alive flared inside Melanie's chest, quickly to be quashed with terror. Had her mother lost her footing? Melanie dared a quick look back.

Her mother and father lagged several yards behind her. Weak, unfit, they struggled to keep up, the bridge of crows bending horribly beneath their weight.

But it wasn't the unsteady bridge that had caused Fumiko's cry of fear.

On an upcrest of the bridge, Melanie could see the hopping, leap-frogging forms of creatures chasing after them. Much faster than her unkempt parents, they were almost upon them. If the crows broke apart, her parents would tumble into the abyss with them.

A sob escaped her lips.

Melanie kept on running. A cool, distant part of her mind

finally understood Jade Rat's abandonment. It seemed so long ago. It was very clear. Her thoughts clicked like clockwork, as her body shifted to automatic. Even if she turned back she could not support her parents' weight, stop them from falling.

Then four people would die instead of two. Two . . .

The creatures that chased them.

They wanted Baby G.

Give them what they want. Throw them the baby. What did it matter? To do one small evil to save the lives of three innocents? They had done nothing to deserve this life! Baby G could grow up into Mr. Glueskin again.

But then it all would start once more. Locking all the Realms into the cycles of suffering.

Throw him into the abyss.

The keen wind shrieking like a shrike, Melanie wrestled with her conflicting thoughts, her writhing feelings.

She ran. She ran.

The mountainside that had seemed so far away loomed, sudden and inexplicable. Like the time travel of dreams. As simple as cool solidity beneath the sole of her foot. She had reached the safety of the ledge. And Baby G was still in her arms. The bulge of relief that filled her chest felt like a bursting heart.

She lowered the baby so he lay in the crook of her arm. Silent so long, was he even alive? Maybe he had been overjostled and killed.

Baby G stared up at her with the certainty of innocence. His large dark eyes were more beautiful than she could bear.

The reality of solid rock brought home the raw panic of falling. Melanie backed to the rock face, the ledge littered with small, dry, brittle bones. They crumped into dust beneath her feet.

Hope and dread formed a chimera inside her, clawing at her throat as if it were trying to birth itself into the world.

Hair whipping in the wind, the rushing roar of thousands upon thousands of wings, Melanie held Baby G in her arms, her feet planted, a fierce look upon her face.

She looked across the divide for her parents.

The bridge had bowed low with their weight. As the Half Worlders raced down to reach them, Fumiko and Shinobu clambered up toward the ledge. No longer able to stand, they were on all fours, scrambling, grasping at the brave birds with their hands, as if they were desperately trying to run up a scree. They clasped each fluttering crow with their hands, their feet pedaling upon a stream of birds that perpetually fell away.

Fumiko's and Shinobu's harsh rasping breath. Their throats raw with terror.

The crows bore them, silent, as each bird, squeezed by hands, pounded with desperate feet, dropped into the abyss like a stone.

Fumiko and Shinobu panted, frantic. The crows—they could not raise them any higher. They were trapped, trying to climb upward, but only injuring crow after crow, without gaining any distance.

The bird-headed man had almost reached them. Close behind was the woman with eel arms. She stuck out her black eel tongue with a lewd grin. A boy-headed dog, as big as a wolf, scampered close to her heels, a monkey with an old man's face clinging to the fur of his back. The bone people clattered close behind.

The crow bridge would scatter at any moment.

Melanie dropped the remnants of Jade Rat on top of the baby

and slammed her palm against the flat rock face. "Gatekeeper!" she screamed. "Gatekeeper! Come out now! Be more than your role! You can make a difference by choosing to act instead of doing your duty," she cried hoarsely. "Change the cycle!" She smacked the stone so hard the small bones of her hand were on the verge of breaking. "Help us now! Choose!" Melanie's voice cracked. Her eyes were squeezed tight with rage, despair. To be this close! It wasn't fair! It wasn't right! She pounded and pounded until her palm was raw, numb, so at first she didn't notice that the rock wall was moving.

With a great groan the giant Gatekeeper wrenched free of her prison and the mountain shook, stones falling from high above, bouncing painfully off the top of Melanie's head. The ledge lurched and Melanie staggered, seeking to regain her balance, even as she hunched over to shelter the baby's exposed face.

Creaking with the weight of tons upon tons of stone, the giant stiffly turned toward the edge of the cliff and swung her arm like a heavy pendulum. Her great rocky hand swooped below the lip of the ledge and plucked Fumiko and Shinobu from their perpetual fall.

The giant gently set them upon the rock ledge and they pressed themselves against the hard surface, almost prone, as if they could still feel gravity yanking them downward.

The crows shrieked with release, with mourning, with exultation. They burst free of their formation, and the Half Worlders cried out in a single voice as they hung in empty air for an eternal moment.

They tumbled down, down, becoming smaller and smaller until they disappeared.

Melanie stared, throat dry. Heart pounding. Her parents still clung to the stone ledge as if it were a life raft in a storm.

The Gatekeeper was not looking into the abyss. Her stone eyes, the same color as her body, gazed implacably at the horizon where a gray light shone.

But the giant had chosen; she had taken action. . . . "Thank you." Melanie's voice was as dry as sand. "From every bit of my heart. I thank you."

The giant looked down, her neck grinding. She stared at Melanie, her expression utterly unreadable.

Melanie gulped. Why did she stare so? Her ears began to grow warm with embarrassment. Why would stone need to blink at all, idiot? she admonished herself.

The giant slowly nodded her chin in acknowledgment.

Baby G still in her arms, Melanie crouched beside her huddled parents. "Shhhhh," Melanie soothed. "It's okay. We made it. It's going to be fine." A warm light swelled inside her and hot tears trickled down her dirty cheeks. Somehow they had made it! "See. We're on the ledge. We just have to go through the portal and we'll be back home! Together!"

Fumiko looked up first. Shuddering, she forced herself to gaze back upon the frightening divide long enough to see that the Half Worlders were truly gone and that the last remnants of the bridge of crows were distant specks of black in a pale gray sky.

Relief bloomed across her face and she finally smiled, calm as moonlight. She tugged Shinobu's arm so that he sat up. Together, they bowed their gratitude to the Gatekeeper who had plucked them from an eternal fall.

"Come on!" Melanie cried. "Let's go home!" She glanced at Baby G. Exhausted, he had fallen asleep, his chubby hand clutching the red strings of the broken jade amulet. She did not see her parents looking at each other. Shinobu stroking Fumiko's hair gently. Reassuringly.

They rose and drew Melanie toward them so her back was pressed near their chests. She could feel the strong thumping of their hearts. Fumiko and Shinobu placed a hand upon each of her shoulders as they tilted their heads back to meet the Gatekeeper's implacable eyes.

"Melanie and the infant seek passage to the Realm of Flesh," Fumiko uttered in a steady voice.

"Wha—" Melanie began.

"You must pay the toll," the Gatekeeper groaned.

"What!" Melanie whipped her face from the Gatekeeper to her mother. "What do you mean! I came to get you! You can't abandon me!" Fear, anger, began to writhe in her chest. She glared at the giant. "You helped us! Can't you just open the Gate? Don't make us pay the toll again!" She was breathing hard, her feelings growing large and monstrous.

"Breathe slowly," Shinobu said gently.

"Shut up!" Melanie shouted. "Shut up! You've never been in my life before! Why would I start listening to you now! You're not my father! You never were!"

Shinobu smiled a trembling smile. "You're right," he answered softly. "I wasn't there. I am sorry for that. To have missed you growing into such a remarkable young woman." He shook his head with regret. "I am so grateful that you came across to help your mother. That I got to see you, even if it's only this one time."

His calm voice deflated her rage as quickly as it had flared.

The terror she felt was worse.

She dragged her aching hand across her eyes. "Mummy," she implored. "Mummy!"

Tears welled in Fumiko's eyes. Her smudged eyeliner looked tawdry and cheap. But her voice was strong. Clear. "Your father and I cannot return to the Realm of Flesh. We are not Flesh. We never were. We cannot live there, with our Half Lives. I think I was able to cross into the Realm only because I carried you: I carried Life. And I was able to live a kind of Half Life because I was near you these fourteen years. But I was already fading. I would have faded into nothing if I had stayed any longer."

Melanie rubbed her tearing eyes with the back of her hand, quickly, angrily. "Then I'll stay here!" She gulped at the enormity of what it meant. "I can get used to it...." Her voice trailed off.

Her mother and father were both shaking their heads.

"It cannot be," Fumiko said. "You have Life, as does this infant. This is a condition that cannot be argued. If you willfully break the cycle you disrupt the natural patterns. And no good can come from that. Look at what the division of the Realms has created. Creatures like Mr. Glueskin. Worlds decaying, deteriorating, violence and monstrosity. And we do not even know if Spirits still exist; they have been cut away from us for so many millennia. Melanie, you must go back to the Realm of Flesh. For the good of all things."

"I don't care about the good of all things!" Melanie shouted. "What about the good things for Melanie! And the Realms are already a mess! Why should I worry about my actions making it worse? How much worse can it get? Who cares anyway! We just live our stupid pathetic lives and then we die." She began to sob. "We just die, and I'll die alone. With no one."

Melanie bawled. For all that never was, all that she had hoped for and would never happen. She bawled for the child she could no longer be.

Fumiko and Shinobu and the giant silently bore witness to her pain.

In time Melanie's sobs grew quieter, shuddering now and then for air, until they, too, ended.

She felt empty. She had cried everything away. She felt clean, though her face felt dry and tight from the salt of her tears. Melanie opened her eyes to see that Baby G was staring up at her, his large dark eyes looking sad and wise, the remnants of Jade Rat still tightly clutched in his tiny fist.

He must be getting cold, Melanie thought. I should cover him with something. I hope he doesn't pee on me. . . . She almost smiled.

She felt her mother's hand cup her cheek with aching tenderness. "You're the best thing that's happened to me for all time!" Fumiko said fiercely. "Never forget that. Never doubt it."

Melanie nodded slowly.

"It's time," Fumiko said. Her voice was firm, but Melanie could feel her mother's fingers trembling.

Melanie spun around. She thrust Baby G at Shinobu and flung her arms around her beloved mother. She held her, hard, despite the shards of mirror adorning her mother's dress.

"I love you," Melanie whispered fiercely.

"Melanie." Fumiko's voice wobbled. But she caught her breath, and when she began speaking once more she was filled with certainty. "I will love you through all time, from across every Realm, for eternity. My love will be near you wherever you go. You are not alone. I promise you this!"

Melanie could not answer. She did not dare try to speak now. Her father returned Baby G to her arms. He raised both hands to cup her face, but stopped before contact. "May I?" he asked humbly.

Melanie nodded once more and her father cupped her chin with his palms and kissed her tenderly on top of her sweaty and dirty hair.

She felt suffused with love.

"The toll must be paid or the portal will not open," the giant intoned, her voice deeply regretful.

Melanie bit her lip. She did not think she could do it. The thought alone filled her with dread. It was so stupid, she thought. She just ran across an abyss over a bridge of flying crows. But that had been in panicked desperation. To do something like amputate your own finger, soberly, as a conscious act . . .

Fumiko tugged off the long gloves she was still wearing. She did it so quickly Melanie did not have time to say the words to stop her.

The wet crunch came sudden and awful and Shinobu turned his head to the side.

Black blood stained Fumiko's teeth. She spat out her second pinkie onto the rocky ledge. "Do you accept this toll?" she asked, her voice shaking.

"Mother," Melanie whispered.

The giant backed away from them, and with the grinding of a great millstone, a crescent cracked the cliff wall and slowly widened into a circle.

NINETEEN

MELANIE'S HEART QUIETED into a small dark knot. It was a dense and hibernating seed. She would keep it so. It felt much better this way. She did not say anything further, but lowered her head and stepped through the hole in the mountain wall with Baby G warm inside her arms.

Her back leg, then foot, passed through the portal, and she left Half World behind.

A sound that was not sound, a motion that could not be felt, like silent waves, expanding outward in ever-widening rings. Like the biggest, largest, thickest bell tolling in a night sky, the sound so low, so deep it could not be discerned by human ears, the Realms rang with such immeasurable force Melanie felt like she would blow apart into atoms.

"Oh!" Melanie heard her parents gasp as if from a great distance.

Something was happening! Had the Gatekeeper turned on them?

Sudden fear filled Melanie's heart. She had not thought about how her parents would cross back to the other side of the abyss....

She did not want to look, to have to witness her parents' final suffering. But she could not stop herself.

On the other side of the portal her mother and father stood, staring down at their own arms, eyes widened.

Not with fear, but wonder . . .

Their black-and-white bodies—their Half Life flesh—were beginning to glow from within. Seams and cracks of light appeared in their exposed skin, her mother glowing dark red, her father a cool lavender. Melanie, terrified, stared at their faces for signs of pain. But only wonder filled their faces, and deep contentment. As if they were in the most warm and comforting bath, when they had gone their entire lives without.

"Ohhhh," they sighed. They turned to look upon their daughter, profound gratitude, awe, respect emanating from their faces.

"It is done," Fumiko sighed. Red tears of light streamed from her eyes, as dark and rich as glowing embers. "My darling girl. You have done it."

Fumiko and Shinobu closed their eyes, and the matter of their bodies broke apart into a thousand motes of red and lavender light.

"Ah!" Melanie gasped.

The motes of light hovered in human shape for several seconds before they began to flutter like a shower of cherry blossom petals falling from a tree. But instead of falling to the ground they shimmered and fluttered upward.

Time had slowed. Perhaps it had stopped. But suddenly the portal began to close with a millstone grinding.

Tears streamed down Melanie's cheeks. She stretched out one hand imploringly.

The crescent of the portal was waning.

Suddenly, several motes of her mother's dark red light flew away from the cluster that continued to rise upward. They flew apart then spiraled together to form a single larger ball of light. The dark red *hinotama*, her mother's soul, no larger than a chickadee, darted through the last sliver of the portal before it closed. With a great groan the entrance to Half World was lost.

The red light zipped and darted in the sudden grayness. It spun dizzy circles around Melanie, shot straight up, and plunged down into Melanie's arms.

It seemed to splash into Baby G.

The light disappeared.

Melanie was numb.

Why hadn't that part of her mum gone into her? Why did she choose the baby?

It was done. That was what her mother had said.

Melanie felt a thousand years old.

Everything was gray. A mist, a fog, wherever it was, it was less a world than Half World. It wouldn't even count as an eighth, Melanie thought. She was so exhausted. Of everything. There was a baby in her arms and it was growing heavy. It would be so nice to just lay it down on the ground.

Somehow, she kept on walking in the dense gray mist.

She had come upon a faint and narrow path. Her feet followed the whispery trail that faded in and out of existence. Her footsteps made no sound. She was uncertain why she followed the incomplete path, but there didn't seem to be much else to do. She looked up once, but everything lay shrouded with a heavy mist that was neither wet nor cold. She lowered her eyes. She felt mildly uneasy.

She had forgotten something, but she couldn't recall what it was. The girl felt a small ache in her chest. She glanced down and saw that she carried a sleeping infant whose hands were clasped over his belly. How peculiar, she thought. I'm carrying a baby.

She continued walking. On the path to every nowhere.

She remembered nothing.

She could have been walking for hours. She could have been walking for decades. Only the mild uneasiness inside her chest. Just placing one foot in front of the other.

Something rippled.

Like circular waves expanding outward, the small movement lapped at the girl's body and her consciousness clutched at the change. Laboriously, she slowed her legs' thoughtless motion and ground to a standstill. The path seemed to tug at her spirit, an aching compulsion to continue. She pressed her palm, hard, against her heavy chest. She should just keep walking like the path wanted her to. . . .

The something rippled through the fog once more.

Someone was calling.

She turned around, heavily, as if she were deep underwater, and pain pierced her to the core.

Melanie!

The voice. So familiar. So far away. She could not say where she had heard it before.

In the great noncolor of the mist, Melanie thought she saw a tiny flicker of dark red light. It did not seem to draw much closer. It bobbed rapidly back and forth, as if struggling against a strong current.

Come back.

The voice was tinny, as if coming through an old-fashioned radio.

Melanie's numb thoughts began to thaw. Curiosity threaded through her consciousness and she began to wonder. Was someone back there, holding a candle?

A second flame flickered beside the first. A cool lavender orb. Then a third and a fourth.

Melanie! Melanie!

Several voices called, and the sound drew tears to her eyes. Straining with the last of her strength, Melanie took one faltering step toward the lights. Pain ripped through Melanie's chest as she resisted the path's beckoning, but the pain cleared her dulled senses.

Half World.

Her parents lost. Turned into light. Gone. Melanie left alone. With Baby G . . .

"I don't want to remember," Melanie whispered.

Senseless. To have lost all that she had ever known—lost what had been most precious to her . . . All the struggle and heartache, all for nothing. At least nothing left for her . . .

And where was she now? Dead or alive. Or something else. Where did the path lead?

She wanted to lie down and sleep for a long time. She was tired of running from danger. She was tired of heartbreak. She was just tired.

The fog billowed encouragingly around her ankles. It crept up her thighs, leaching the last reservoirs of self-will she had remaining.

Come back! The voices called again, thin and faded. *We can't reach you on our own. You have to meet us halfway!*

Melanie wanted so much to close her eyes.

Why should she bother going back to her world after all that had happened? There was nothing to return to.

What if there is? A tiny voice inside her asked. What if there might be?

Melanie teetered on the cusp.

Let go, the fog invited. It lapped around her knees, swirled gently around her torso, its numbing touch ever so slightly soft and so blessedly muffling. Forget everything, the fog said seductively, and you'll finally find peace.

Peace, Melanie thought dreamily. Peace would be very sweet.

As if sensing her capitulation the fog swelled almost gleefully, clasping, clutching at her limbs, engulfing her. Creeping toward her face.

Melanie! the voices called urgently. They sounded far more distant than they had before. She opened her eyes, and the tiny lights seemed like fragile candles burning in a stormy night. Forget, the fog seemed to whisper. Sending gentle tendrils toward her face. Peace forever.

There was a flutter in her arms. The baby was gazing up at her with large dark eyes. He fluttered his feet once more.

Dead meant no longer alive in the world she'd been born into. The world she had been trying so desperately to return to with her parents.

Half World hadn't offered peace for anyone she'd seen there. And who knew what the Spirits did in their Realm?

To have lost all that she had known and loved so dearly . . . was there life, still, after that?

A tiny flame flickered inside her.

Yes, it said. Yes.

Melanie tried to raise one foot, to take a step toward the voices that called. They sounded familiar. She wanted to know who they were.

The fog writhed wildly, almost hissing as it tried to bind her. Melanie bore down hard, slogging through the thick tendrils. They clung to her arms and legs, and she forced her way through them as if tearing away from vines. She groaned at the weight, the numbing spell the fog tried to weave, but she took another step and inched a little closer to the voices that had called her name.

The weighty fog focused upon her neck. It clenched and squeezed, pulling her back to the place of despair and exhaustion it had wrought.

Melanie dug in, and reached deep inside herself. To that small, hidden place where she was so completely Melanie there was room for nothing else. Where she was as hard as carbon and more brilliant than a diamond.

The fog squealed and screamed as it tried to pour into her nostrils, ears, and mouth. Melanie refused. She clung to herself and believed. Hope swelled inside her chest and broke free, streaming from her body in bright rays of light.

The fog gibbered away, and in its wake Melanie found herself standing on loamy ground. It was slightly spongy, and the smell of peat and soil was richly brown. Although she could see, she could not pinpoint a source of light. It was as if she were in and among light though nothing shone.

Four orbs of fire, the size of two cupped palms, zigzagged and swirled toward her. Ember red, pale lavender, dark green, and sea-shell pink, the *hinotama* were warm as breath, cool as an evening breeze. They danced around Melanie's head, swooping in to rain light kisses upon her upturned face, and she was suffused with sweet happiness.

TWENTY

MELANIE, A VOICE said wonderingly. Proudly. *You did it.*

Melanie blinked back a sudden surge of tears. "Mother?" she asked. "Is that you?"

Yes, the Spirit answered.

And Melanie realized she wasn't exactly hearing the words. She could sense them, and the memory of the voice followed.

The Realms are reunited. The binding has been broken! a childish voice bubbled excitedly. She sounded familiar.

Melanie blinked with growing joy. "Are you the starfish-child?"

The pink light spun in dizzy circles, flying figure eights with joyful glee. *Yes! Yes! Yes! I'm free!*

Oh, Melanie, Shinobu's voice murmured. *You saved us all.*

We, so long trapped in Half World, have become Spirits. The dark green light hovered in front of Melanie's face.

"Gao Zhen Xi," Melanie sighed. "You, too."

Yes, her familiar voice said warmly. *I thank you with all my Spirit. You are a wonder.*

"I don't know," Melanie said in a small voice. "What's going to happen to me? Am I dead?"

No, Fumiko's Spirit said firmly. *You have not lived out your life's path.*

"Can't I stay with you?" Melanie whispered.

Oh, Melanie, Fumiko's Spirit sighed. *I know it's hard to live. If I could but return with you to the Realm of Flesh. But if I did it would undo all that you have done to reunite the divided Realms. There is balance in the Realms once more. But this balance has been reached while you have suffered loss. Believe that you have a life still waiting for you in the Realm of Flesh and with that life all that is possible and yet to be. I know you'll find joy again. You brought joy to so many. The Realm of Spirits has been filled with the light of those who've been trapped in Half World for too long. Joy will come back to you.*

"Can you promise me?" Melanie asked.

The four *hinotama* pulled back simultaneously. They hovered before her, minute variations to their light. Dark green flames, flickers of seashell pink, threads of pale lilac inside a lavender fire, and the dark, warm depth of red in her mother's Spirit.

There are never guarantees in life, Gao Zhen Xi's Spirit said sternly. Her "voice" softened. *But for those who strive, who dream and believe, live with an open heart, and dare to love, it is almost certain that joy will come to you.*

"That's a lot to ask, to live like that. I don't know if I can anymore. I don't know if I want to." A shiver crawled up Melanie's spine. She could feel the oppressive weight of the fog waiting for her to despair.

It is for you to choose what you will do with your life. Rest, if you are weary. Hide, when it is prudent to do so. But try to live it fully. Live as you are meant to live! Her mother's Spirit was jubilant. *Darling girl! What you have done! Know that the actions of one girl can change everything!*

A shiver of wind. Like leaves rustling. The scent of green and growing things. The *hinotama* floated upward, like ashes above a fire. Melanie did not know if they were rising high above her or if they were simply shrinking. Baby G raised a pudgy hand as if to bat at the beautiful glowing lights. Suddenly, they arced across the sky like shooting stars.

They were gone.

The rustling grew a little louder, verging on the edge of a soft roar.

Leaves. Small silvery leaves glinted on slender boughs. The sudden breeze smelled slightly bitter and sweet, like sap in the spring.

Melanie stood in a glade of young aspens in the middle of a pristine vale. Growing here and there were small clusters of young, leafy trees, and brilliant stars lit up the night skies in oddly shaped constellations, though a light seemed to be growing, from which direction she couldn't say. Time seemed to hover between dusk and dawn. The air smelled green.

She inhaled deeply and the air tasted delicious.

Her heart felt lighter.

Baby G twisted inside her arms. When a cool breeze skated over his skin he began to shiver.

Melanie frowned. She looked around but could see nothing she could use. She set the baby down on the soft grass and quickly tore several feet of cloth from the bottom of her dress. She awkwardly bundled up the infant.

Baby G gurgled with satisfaction.

What place had she come to now?

It certainly wasn't Half World. But it didn't smell like her own Realm, either.

Which way should she go, to find the way back home?

One direction seemed have begun glowing a little brighter. She turned toward the light, when her foot snagged on something hard and she almost fell. Staggering, hopping as she struggled not to fall upon the baby, Melanie finally regained her balance.

"Ouch," she said belatedly. She rubbed the raw top of her foot against the back of her calf.

What was that?

It didn't feel like the nature stuff in the rest of the glowing glade.

It was definitely growing lighter, because she could see more details. There was something sticking out of the grass.

It looked like a metal handle.

Melanie tilted her head with thought. She experimentally tapped the ground with her heel.

A hollow sound.

Melanie knelt beside the metal handle and ran her fingers around the flat surface. Square in shape, it was a trapdoor made of wood. She experimentally pulled at the handle.

It was stuck fast.

Melanie moved Baby G several feel away from the trapdoor, then grabbed the handle with both hands. She heaved and strained, her temples almost bursting with the effort, until the seal began to give. She released her hold and took several deep breaths. Then she pulled firmly but carefully once more.

The trapdoor suddenly popped open and fell out of her hands just as a vast, stinking beast roared in the space beneath her, clouds of black exhaust billowing upward.

"AH!" Melanie shouted and kicked the door shut with her foot.

Her heart pounded until the smell of the terrible clouds filtered into her consciousness.

Exhaust.

The exhaust from a vehicle.

Could it be?

Melanie crouched beside the hatch, pried it up, and held it partially open.

Directly below them, around fifteen feet away, was a strip of broken white lines painted onto concrete. A dingy orange light cut through a film of automobile exhaust.

The roof of a small sedan whipped past, followed by a dark pickup truck.

Melanie's eyes widened.

She was *above* the Cassiar Tunnel.

But not on Adanac Street, where she and Ms. Wei had stood so very long ago. This was a different place. Something new and growing . . .

She gazed once more at the perfect glade, so separate from the din and pollution beneath her. She looked through the hatch for the way back to her noisy and messy world.

Attached to the wall directly below the hatch was a small metal ladder. She could just make out a sign beside it near the bottom. SECONDARY EMERGENCY EXIT, it read. Sighing, Melanie clutched Baby G awkwardly to her chest. She took one last deep draft of the perfectly green-smelling air of her special glade.

Maybe, one day, she would be able to find it once again.

Melanie lowered her feet onto the rungs of the metal ladder. It felt disgusting on her bare toes, sticky, tarry with exhaust fumes and particles of oil. She curled her toes around the metal and stuck her free arm deep, so that she gripped the rung with the inside of her elbow. Using her elbow to hold her weight, she inched downward with her feet, almost dangling, as she held Baby G in her other arm.

Just imagine, Melanie thought. To make it through Half World and come back home only to fall off a ladder in the Cassiar Tunnel. It would have been hilarious if it weren't so precarious.

The occasional vehicle whipped by. No one seemed to notice the young woman crawling down the inside wall of the tunnel. Melanie prayed that she wouldn't be passed by a semitrailer. The tailwinds would certainly suck her to her death.

Panting, keening from the pain in her elbow, Melanie made her awkward way down, Baby G keeping very still the entire way.

When her feet touched the firmness of concrete she almost wept with joy.

A driver caught her in the corner of his eye. The sound of the horn blared, amplified in the confines of the concrete tunnel.

Melanie's heart plugged her throat.

She coughed in the aftermath of the exhaust.

Baby G was coughing as well. She had to hurry and get out of the poisonous air.

Melanie walked out of the garish orange lighting of the Tunnel onto the freeway.

It was night.

She had no idea what day it was.

For all that she knew, time might have passed by more quickly, here. Who could say?

Melanie's eyes were dry. Her throat ached. Her feet were growing cold. Yes, it had been autumn when she first left her Realm.
She remembered that. She had come here with Ms. Wei so very
long ago.

Ms. Wei . . .

Something warm began to grow inside her chest.

She would go to Ms. Wei's store. Knock on her door. Ms. Wei
would let her in.

Melanie began tottering down the side of the freeway. She
didn't realize she was on the verge of collapse. That with each step
she took she was that much closer to falling.

A white car whipped past and slammed on its brakes, screeching wildly. It swerved a little as it hit a patch of gravel when it
pulled onto the narrow triangle of pavement between the freeway and the feeder ramp.

The slam of a car door. Pounding footsteps.

The cops, Melanie thought dully. Oh, well. They could take her
and Baby G to Social Services. She was an orphan now. They both
were. It didn't matter.

A rough hand circled her back. It was enough to make Melanie topple. An arm stopped her forward fall and also plucked the
baby from her.

Melanie had not realized how heavy the baby was until he was
gone.

She looked groggily at her captor.

Ms. Wei's worried face glared back, fierce with concern, eyes
intently searching her face. When the old woman saw that Melanie's Life was still in her eyes, her expression softened. "Melanie

has come home," Ms. Wei said wonderingly. "Ms. Wei knew it! Ms. Wei called a cab and came as soon as she knew! Come! Come!" She nudged Melanie to the cab and helped her inside.

It was warm. Smelled like artificial air freshener.

Melanie sagged as the weariness hit her like a sledgehammer.

"Listen, lady," the cabdriver said excitedly, "I can't take you any farther so pay me my fare! You make me stop at a place like this! You didn't say nothing about a baby! There's no baby seat, 'kay! I could lose my license!"

"Silence!" Ms. Wei bellowed. "This girl has saved taxi driver's life and Ms. Wei's life and the lives of everyone in Three Realms! So say nothing about licenses, fool! Drive Ms. Wei back home this instant!"

Cowed, the cabdriver hunched his shoulders protectively around his ears. He glanced at them in the rearview mirror. "Crazies," he muttered. "You better pay me!" he added indignantly.

Ms. Wei turned to Melanie as the car roared forward. "Close Melanie's eyes. Rest for now."

The warmth from the heater seeped into Melanie's aching limbs. Her taut muscles relaxing, she felt like a puddle of water.

It felt so good. To let go.

She—

TWENTY-ONE

MELANIE DID NOT know if it was the knocking that woke her up or the rich smell of something delicious.

Thunk, thunk, thunk, thunk, thunk. The sound came again.

Something was bubbling. She could hear the *buku buku* sound of a savory simmer.

The babbling chortle of a contented baby.

Melanie had no idea where she was.

Her head felt sluggish and empty at the same time. A yellow light shone through a window. She was lying on a bed, underneath a heavy comforter, in a filthy, ragged white dress, with soiled feet.

What a mess she had made of the clean, crisp sheets! Her flare of concern was immediately swamped by her exhaustion. She lay flat atop the mattress like a jellyfish on land. Well, it was done with anyway.

It was done with....

Her mother had said that. *It is done.*

Melanie stared at the ceiling.

Of course.

She had made it back, and somehow Ms. Wei had known to come and pick her up.

This time, a knock came on the door.

"Come in," Melanie rasped.

Ms. Wei nudged backward into the room. She carried a tray that had four legs. Numerous small bowls and plates clattered, and the most enticing aromas filled the small room.

Melanie's stomach rumbled loudly. She sat up and yelped at the stiff pain that sang out all over her body.

"A hot bath would help." Ms. Wei narrowed her eyes. "Which first? Food or bath?"

"Food!" Melanie cried eagerly. "Please," she added. She slowly shifted back against the headrest and patted the quilt flat upon her legs.

Ms. Wei set the tray on the bed, and Melanie's eyes fairly popped out of her head with delight.

The old woman began pointing to each dish. "Congee," she said sternly. "Good for convalescence. Easy to digest and warms the Spirit. Clear chicken broth. Mustard greens. Egg tofu. Steamed sole. Only a little bit! Chrysanthemum greens. Jasmine tea. And"—her voice softened—"a little bit of cake." She smiled and her eyes disappeared into happy creases. "Eat!" She frowned, stern once more. "Not too fast!"

Melanie nodded. She picked up the bowl of congee and the ceramic spoon. A sprinkling of chopped green onions garnished the top. She scooped a small portion into her mouth, and the gentle savory flavors, subtle but rich, were marvelous. Salty, a hint of ginger and the rice slow-cooked until it was mealy and sweet. Her stomach squeezed painfully and she eagerly spooned another mouthful. A third and a fourth.

She lowered the congee and picked up chopsticks. It was so difficult to choose! So many little plates of food.

"Just a little bit at first," Ms. Wei explained. "It startles the stomach if one eats too suddenly after nothing at all. After this small meal Melanie can have a proper supper later."

Melanie chewed on the pungent, slightly bittersweet stem of the mustard green. There were so many layers of taste and smell. If she closed her eyes the flavors were like sculptures upon her palate.

Melanie stopped chewing. "What time is it?" she asked.

"It's eleven in the morning," Ms. Wei said gently. "But of the second day. Melanie slept through the night and the entire next day. Today is Melanie's third day back."

Melanie swallowed. "Oh," she said. "Wow."

"So tired," Ms. Wei sighed.

Melanie nibbled on the steamed egg tofu. She looked around the room, slightly confused. She couldn't stop feeling that there was something missing. . . .

"The baby!" she gasped.

"Shhhhh, shhhh," Ms. Wei said reassuringly. "The baby is fine. Ms. Wei had supplies from the market and he's no worse for wear. He slept as much as Melanie did! And lucky for Ms. Wei, who is too old to be getting up all hours to feed an infant."

"I'm sorry," Melanie said. She looked down at the tray. "He's not your baby to take care of. . . . " She frowned. "But he's not mine, either."

"This is so." Ms. Wei nodded thoughtfully. "Well! Eat first. Melanie has much to tell. But there is no rush. Eat. Bathe. Then

Melanie will tell a tale from the comfortable chair by the window. In the sunshine."

Melanie's chin suddenly wobbled. "Yes," she quavered. Smiled. "That's a good idea." She took a nibble of the steamed fish.

She had never had such a fish in her entire life. "Ms. Wei," she said solemnly, "this is the best meal I have ever eaten. Thank you very much."

"Ahhh!" Ms. Wei exclaimed, flapping her hand with embarrassment. "This is nothing! When Melanie is better Ms. Wei will make a great steamed lobster!"

The autumn afternoon sun enfolded Melanie in a cozy cocoon of warmth. Melanie sat in one of the two easy chairs beside the west window, a blanket draped over her legs, her feet in soft slippers. The angle of the sun made long shadows stripe Ms. Wei's living/workroom. The motes of dust caught in the bars of light shone like gold. In the distance Melanie could see the inlet and the bright orange cranes of the wharfs, looking like a herd of mechanical giraffes.

Melanie stared wonderingly out the window. The colors of her Realm were so remarkable. She could not get over how many shades of green existed in one laurel bush. She had forgotten the depths, the multihued, vibrant shades of Life.

Had she ever noticed?

The nuances of moss, rich and lush upon the trunks of trees that lined the block. The coarse umbers of bark, highlighted with gray-blue lichen. Invisible birds twittered in a mess of blackberry brambles in an empty lot across the street. In front of the co-op apartment building a few doors down, a camellia was blooming its deep pink flowers, their yellow centers a miracle of brightness. She stared, mesmerized, at the cars that whizzed past, their tires splashing through small puddles of water. The vehicles seemed remarkable, marvelous in ridiculously bright shades of red, yellow, teal green, cobalt blue. The colors zinged into her brain as if they were sound, and the symphony was simply glorious.

Melanie took a deep breath.

It was so good to be still.

How beautiful, Life . . .

A gurgling mutter. A series of gasping breaths. A great nasal wail cracked the stillness of the afternoon.

Holy crow! Melanie thought, eyes wide at the sheer volume of the baby's cry. Before she could stand she heard footfalls *tack, tack, tack*ing up the wooden stairs, and Ms. Wei burst into the room.

"Yaaaaah!" Ms. Wei exclaimed. "Isn't Baby so noisy? Ms. Wei never had children for a reason and almost had to break up with Nora Stein, Spirits bless her now and always, because of it. And now baby comes into the house in Ms. Wei's old age! Nora Stein's Spirit must be laughing! Isn't life unknowable!" The old woman ran to heat a bottle of milk in the kitchen and snatched up a cloth diaper and baby wipes on the way back.

The baby was in a bassinet underneath the ornamental orange tree. Bawling loudly. Like he was normal . . .

Melanie watched as Ms. Wei efficiently changed the diaper and carried the baby with her to the kitchen for the warmed bottle.

"How do you know how to take care of babies?" Melanie asked. "If you and Nora Stein didn't have one?"

Ms. Wei sat in the second easy chair with the crying infant in her arms. She slipped the nipple of the baby bottle into the baby's eager mouth.

"Ahhhhh," Melanie and Ms. Wei both sighed as it became quiet once more.

Melanie looked at him. There were teardrops stuck in his eyelashes and his eyelids began drooping with satisfaction as he sucked the formula hungrily.

He looked awfully sweet, Melanie thought.

"Ms. Wei helped her mother raise siblings," Ms. Wei explained in a quiet voice. "Ms. Wei was the oldest and had eight sisters and brothers."

"Eight!" Melanie exclaimed.

"Yes. Eight strong, smart, stubborn siblings. By the time Ms. Wei was sixteen years old she had had her fill of infants, cute though they are." Ms. Wei stared down at the drowsy baby. "What's this one's name?"

"I've been thinking of him as Baby G," Melanie admitted. "He used to be Mr. Glueskin, the evil thing that was tormenting my parents! But he was born again. I don't think he's the same any-more."

"Hohhhhh." Ms. Wei nodded.

They listened to the hungry sucking of the baby. The after-noon sun was warm and comforting.

"Ms. Wei?" Melanie finally asked.

"Hmmm?"

"Do you think Baby G will be okay, now?"

Ms. Wei looked up, her forehead slightly furrowed.

"What I mean is—" Melanie's voice cracked. She cleared her throat and swallowed hard. "What if he turns into Mr. Glueskin again? Only here. In our Realm instead," she whispered anxiously.

Ms. Wei stared at Melanie for several seconds, then shifted her gaze to the baby.

Baby G's eyes were closed. He was frowning with concentration as he focused on draining the bottle of formula. His cheeks were flushed rosy with warmth and his two chubby fists were clenched.

He smelled like milk and baby powder.

A slight whistling sound. Baby G had finished the bottle and was sucking only air. Ms. Wei pulled the nipple out of his mouth and raised him to her shoulder. She began gently patting his back.

"Rest easy," Ms. Wei said gently. "Baby G is no longer trapped in Half World. He is at the beginning of something else. In a new cycle. He cannot become the Glueskin that Melanie knew. That cycle is broken."

Baby G gave a long, low burp. Then he farted.

Melanie could not help but giggle.

They sat in silence for several minutes. Just the soothing tap, tapping of Ms. Wei's gentle hand on Baby G's back.

A thought occurred to Melanie. "How did you know to come pick me up? At just the right time?"

Ms. Wei's eyes widened dramatically. "That night! All the newborn babies. Every single one of them in the entire world. They all began to cry at the same time! Ms. Wei could hear them in the neighborhood, the noise filling the entire city. It lasted a few minutes. Then it stopped! Then, it appeared on Ms. Wei's table!"

Melanie blinked, confused. "What appeared on the table?" Did she mean one of the babies who had cried?

Ms. Wei gestured with her chin, because she was still hold-ing the baby. "Go! If Melanie has enough strength. Look on the table."

Melanie couldn't stop the groan of pain when she rose to her feet. Every muscle in her body ached and throbbed and she awk-wardly hobbled to the table.

A bar of golden light cast a beautiful glow upon the grand dark cherry-red tabletop. Ms. Wei had cleared all of her research clutter from the surface.

There was only a single book.

It looked ancient, the cover blackened and cracked with age. There was no title or script of any kind, only a slightly embossed circular emblem. It looked like the yin-yang symbol, but instead of two pieces that nestled perfectly together to form a circle of dark and light there were three, the pieces made of black, white, and gray....

Melanie's mouth slowly fell open. "Is that *The Book of the Realms*?" she asked hoarsely.

Ms. Wei solemnly nodded her head. "The writing was like the little scrap of magic paper from my archives!" she whispered. "This book appeared. There was a sound, like a big deep bell, but the sound was silent. It rippled, certainly, across the entire universe."

Melanie slowly nodded her head. She had felt it. Just after her mother's voice had said, *It is done....*

"Ms. Wei read the book while Melanie slept. It told of how the three entwined Realms had become divided and the woes that followed. It spoke of a prophecy of a child, born with Life in a Realm without it. And how a brave girl walked into Half World to face great evil. How she stopped evil, without doing evil herself

"…and in doing so, reunited the divided Realms into balance once more." Ms. Wei's eyes shone with respect and admiration.

Melanie's ears burned. Ms. Wei meant her! The book had told her story. Melanie's heart leapt.

Wait a second, she thought. The book was in the Archives of Unfinished Books … The last one-third had been blank pages.

"Did you finish the book?" Melanie asked hoarsely. "From beginning to end?"

Ms. Wei nodded solemnly. "Ms. Wei has learned so much. Near the end, it explained why all the newborn infants in the world began to cry. It was all of the Spirits who remained, long overdue, finally returning to Flesh. Those in Half World finally became Spirit. And we, in this Realm, are no longer trapped in the limitations of Flesh. Melanie, there is ever much more to understand. Ms. Wei will read this book her entire life to comprehend the interconnected workings of the Realms!"

Melanie thoughtfully stroked the cover of the book. A funny little tingle shot up her fingers. It was not unpleasant.

She did not open it. She was not quite ready to read about her story, as if it were someone else. The experiences were still too close.

She still needed to feel through it all.

Melanie thoughtfully returned to her seat and wrapped the blanket around her legs. She stared out the window. The book, here in this Realm, completed. It was unfinished no longer. All the babies crying … Ms. Wei had said it felt like a great silent bell rang across the universe. It must have been at the same moment when her parents had turned into light. Her mother's deep red light, and her father pale lavender, flying upward …

Melanie pressed her hand to her mouth. "I'm so sorry!" she blurted, as realization and guilt swamped her. "I must have dropped it! And Jade Rat helped me so many times. I wouldn't be here if it hadn't been for Jade Rat. She was your ancestor's companion rat. Her name was Gao Zhen Xi. . . . " Tears began to fill her eyes.

"No, no!" Ms. Wei sounded alarmed. "Melanie must not apologize!" She carried the sleeping baby back to the bassinet. The old woman turned to an ornately carved box on her bookshelf and carefully unwrapped something from a piece of cloth. Ms. Wei returned to the chairs and held out her closed fist.

Melanie, fingers trembling, opened her palm.

The jade amulet felt slightly warm against her skin.

The missing piece that had been broken off in Mr. Glueskin's penthouse had somehow been made whole. The rat and its rough details were intact.

The stone had turned into a deep dark red.

Melanie stared and stared as her thoughts raced back to those last moments. *It is done*, her mother's voice had said. And then a small portion of her mother's light had flown to Baby G and not her.

That part of her mother's Spirit . . . it had not gone into the baby. It had joined the jade amulet, merging with the stone, so that she could return to the Realm of Flesh!

Her mother had kept her promise.

Melanie clamped the amulet against her chest. After several minutes she lowered the stone so that it lay cradled in her palms, upon her lap. Sunbeams shone through the stone, highlighting the ears and nose, the sweep of her tail.

The dark center began to glow. The color was so intense, so much like a burning ember that Melanie had to fight the urge to drop it.

The jade amulet began to shimmer, as if the atoms were breaking free from their bonds. Its matter shivered, and it flared momentarily into a blinding light. When the glare receded, a fur-and-whiskers dark red rat sat very still upon Melanie's palms.

"Oh!" Melanie and Ms. Wei gasped simultaneously.

The rat opened its eyes and stretched, baring her long incisors. She sat up on her haunches and scrubbed her whiskers before briskly stroking over both ears.

Melanie's heart raced. She swallowed hard. "Can you talk?" she whispered hoarsely.

"It takes a while," a droll voice muttered from the floor. "You have no idea what it's like to come back like that for the first time."

"Uh!" Melanie yelped with shock at the unexpected voice. That it came from the ground directly behind her.

"Bad manners!" Ms. Wei said crossly. "Apologize for startling Melanie! Why did not Ms. Wei's mother give her a dog!"

Melanie carefully peered around the back of her cushy chair. In a wedge of shadow, curled around a heat vent, sprawled a fat white cat. He ignored her completely, intently licking the pink pads of his front paw.

"He talks? Like Jade Rat?" Melanie asked. "Is he really an amulet, too?"

"How is anyone 'really' more one thing than another?" the cat scoffed from between his toes. "Is a table 'really' more furniture than wood?"

"Silence, Cat!" Ms. Wei commanded. "If you have nothing helpful to say, turn back to stone, real or not!"

The cat sniffed, and raised his hind leg, straight up, to lick his bum.

Melanie scowled. It seemed like some sort of cat insult. She turned back to gaze upon the dark red rat. "Are you still Jade Rat?" Melanie whispered.

The rat raised her small and eloquent nose and tasted the air. "I am Red Jade now," she answered, her voice slightly raspier than when she had been green.

"White Jade is better," a voice muttered from the floor.

"Che!" Ms. Wei exhaled impatiently. "Some jade pieces should be kept in a box for all time!" She turned to Melanie. "Ignore him. He is a bitter old cat. He is not worth his weight in cat food."

"How quickly they forget," White Cat sighed. "You might be in jail if I hadn't saved you from the police officer. Oh, well. As long as I know for myself the things I've done for you, it is enough. I don't need gratitude. Don't mind me. It's enough just to know that I did my best for you and it helped you and that's all tha—"

"Okay! Okay!" Ms. Wei exclaimed. "Ms. Wei is grateful! Okay? White Cat saved Ms. Wei!"

The cat didn't respond with words, but after a moment's silence a loud purr began filling the room.

The purring, Melanie decided, was even worse. A crooked grin quirked her lips at the mixture of frustration, gratitude, and affection on Ms. Wei's face. The old woman shook her head, then began to chortle.

Melanie felt a small hand clasp the end of her thumb. Red Jade's tiny claws prickled her skin. The rat was staring at her alertly, her long tail curled slightly around her wrist.

Melanie saw the place where she had bitten off her smallest finger. To pay the toll. Melanie's heart clenched almost painfully. She raised Red Jade gently to stroke the rat's side with her cheek. The coarse fur tickled.

"Oh, Melanie," Red Jade rasped. "I remember."

EPILOGUE

THE STREET LAMPS *shone orange cones of light against the mistiness of night. Most of the homes, apartment buildings, older-model duplexes were dark, in the quiet stillness of deepest sleep. The city breathed inside dreams and nightmares. In the distance a siren spiraled, the sound signaling the troubles of someone else. A dog in a kennel howled.*

The windows of the Rainbow Market, and in the apartment above, were all dark. A cold breeze blew from the north. The possibility of snow was a sweet metallic flavor in the air.

The night was cracked by the loud nasal wail of a baby.

Several seconds passed as the infant continued crying. A pale rectangle of light flicked on from the second floor of the market. The baby's cries grew louder, and a second smaller rectangle of light, directly beside the first window, was switched on. The glow was brave and warm in the night building. The baby cried and cried for several minutes until the sound began to wane.

The lights remained on, but it was silent once more.

Atop the flat gravel-covered roof of the market apartment sat four creatures. The silhouettes of a large, fat cat, a rat, and two crows were framed in the irregular round of a three-quarter moon.

The cat sighed theatrically, his tail twitching with annoyance. "I still think they should get rid of the baby." He sniffed.

The rat whipped her tail to whack the cat's fat rump. The cat yowled indignantly. The two crows rustled their wings, and one gave a low, hoarse caw.

The fur on the cat's nape puffed out threateningly for several seconds, before he let it lie once more.

"Take care with the words you utter," the rat said sternly. "The fate of one baby can alter everything. As you well know!"

The large cat yawned.

The two crows opened wide their beaks and made an odd popping sound.

"So the girl saves the Realms, loses her parents, and ends up living with an old woman while they raise a baby," the white cat said snidely. "Human lives are so pitifully pedestrian. You have to admit it. There is nothing spectacular about them. How awful it must be to be human."

The rat opened wide her mouth and revealed her long incisors in a great rat grin. "Don't be so certain," she said. "Sometimes endings are beginnings in the making."

The two crows tilted their heads to peer with one eye at the rat.

The rat winked, then scampered across the roof to the gutter. The sound of her tiny claws against the metal set the cat yowling.

"What do you mean?" the cat cried out belatedly, indignantly.

But the rat was already inside, in the warmth of the second-floor apartment.

The cat sat up tall, the fur on his tail bristling. "I hate it when she does that," he muttered to himself. Affecting indifference, he ambled casually toward the fire escape stairs to join her.

Only the two whispering crows remained.

Dark clouds moved the moon in and out of light. The heavy moisture in the air crinkled into minute crystals of ice.

On the windows of the second-story apartment, frost began to fern and spiral upon the pane of glass. The light was turned off. In the quiet, in the darkness, the frost bloomed into a forest.

ACKNOWLEDGMENTS

A book, finally completed, is not the result of the efforts of a lone individual but the culmination of the generative energies and interactions between family and community, place and time. This book would not have happened without the support, friendship, and love of so many people.

Foremost, thank you to Sae and Koji. You are the best thing that has happened to me for all time.

Kyoko Goto, thank you so much for telling me that the well would not run dry ... You're right. The well was not empty. Your words kept me from despair.

During the writing and rewriting of this novel my *oba-chan* and my father have moved on to the Realm of Spirit. Thank you for everything that you shared with me. Everything I'm learning, still. I miss you....

I am profoundly grateful to Nozomi Goto and Chris Goto-Jones for generously sharing their home with me and creating a space where I could write—I wouldn't have been able to complete the final draft without this shelter of time. Susanda Yee, for our long conversations and mutual care that sees us through so many realms; I am so lucky to have you in my life. Tortoises rule! (In the long run . . .) Rita Wong, for your long-time support and kind heart. Your fierce and loving advocacy for social justice continues to inspire. Eva Tai, for seeing the essence of the moment and being unafraid to speak it, your words continue to challenge, comfort, and intrigue me. Tamai Kobayashi, thank you for your generous, generous emergency feedback and faith in my work. Chris Goto-Jones, for providing critical plot analysis on the final draft in the eleventh hour—it bridged the chasm between impossible and possible. David Bateman, for the experience of creative collaborations, Pinky cocktails, and enjoying the glamorous moment. Larissa Lai, for your support and quirky humor and razor-sharp mind. Naomi Goto, for your long-time quiet faith in my writing, and Ayumi Goto, for first convincing me to go on an over-a-month-long retreat, something I'd never done before, and taking care of the home front while I was away. Ashok Mathur, for the quiet of your homespace when I needed a break. And Sae Goto, for your feedback during the final read-aloud edit the night before the deadline.

A huge Rah!Rah!Rah! to the Writing Cheerleading Squad who saw me through the very first draft so long ago! Nalo Hopkinson, Pam Mordecai, Jennifer Stevenson, Larissa Lai, Martin Mordecai, thank you for all the encouragement. Here's to seeing each other through many more projects!

So many people have been invaluable at different times during the long process of completing this work. My gratitude to Tamotsu Tongu, Kyo Maclear, Baco Ohama, Aruna Srivastava,

Roy Miki, Cecilia Martell. And a special thank-you to Roseanne Johnson, my counselor: I swear I'm not gonna go Woody Allen on you!

I am grateful to the 2007 Writer-in-Residency Program at the Vancouver Public Library, the Friends of the Library, and the Canada Council for the Arts.

A special thank-you to Jillian Tamaki for the amazing illustrations and the stunning cover art.

My gratitude to Barbara Berson, who first saw what this book might become, and to Leona Trainer, for finding it a home. Jennifer Glossop, you are an editor superhero! Your perceptive eye and thoughtful feedback are greatly appreciated. I am happy that I got to work with you! Thank you to the people at Penguin Group Canada who have been so supportive (and patient!); I am especially grateful to Jennifer Notman, Marcia Gallego, and Tracy Bordian. My heartfelt gratitude to Sharyn November and Viking USA.

Thank you to the crows that amass on Vancouver evenings and fly home to the darkness of Burnaby Mountain. Thank you to the brilliance of wet moss and lichen. Thank you to the rays of golden brown light slanting in the cool of a green lake. Thank you to the shoals of glinting fish. Thank you to the sweet gems of salmonberries. Thank you to the decaying leaves for their rich brown smell. Thank you to the slugs and wood lice beneath the leaves. Thank you to my plant friends who keep me company as I write. I am deeply grateful to share this cycle with you.

HIROMI GOTO was born in Chiba-ken, Japan, and immigrated to Canada with her family in 1969. Her first novel, *Chorus of Mushrooms*, examined the immigration experience and was the 1995 regional winner of the Commonwealth Writers' Prize for Best First Book and cowinner of the Canada-Japan Book Award. She is also the author of *The Kappa Child*, which was the 2001 recipient of the James Tiptree, Jr. Award (www.tiptree.org), a children's novel, *The Water of Possibility*, and, most recently, the short story collection *Hopeful Monsters*.

She lives in Canada. Visit her Web site at www.hiromigoto.com.

JILLIAN TAMAKI grew up on the Canadian prairies (Calgary, Alberta). In addition to her editorial illustration, she co-created a graphic novel, *Skim*, with her cousin Mariko Tamaki; it has received great acclaim, including selection as one of the *New York Times'* Best Illustrated Books.

Jillian Tamaki lives in Brooklyn, New York, with her husband, illustrator Sam Weber. Her Web site is www.jilliantamaki.com.